KU-132-221

CONTENTS

◆

CAMBRIDGE LITERATURE

This edition of *Ethan Frome* is part of the Cambridge Literature series, and has been specially prepared for students in schools and colleges who are studying the book as part of their English course.

This study edition invites you to think about what happens when you read the novel, and it suggests that you are not passively responding to words on the page which have only one agreed interpretation, but that you are actively exploring and making new sense of what you read. Your 'reading' will partly stem from you as an individual, from your own experiences and point of view, and to this extent your interpretation will be distinctively your own. But your reading will also stem from the fact that you belong to a culture and a community, rooted in a particular time and place. So, your understanding may have much in common with that of others in your class or study group.

There is a parallel between the way you read this book and the way it was written. The Resource Notes at the back are devised to help you to investigate the complex nature of the writing process. This begins with the author's first, tentative ideas and sources of inspiration, moves through to the stages of writing, production and publication, and ends with the text's reception by the reading public, reviewers, critics and students. So the general approach to study focuses on five key questions:

Who has written *Ethan Frome* and why?

What type of text is it?

How was *Ethan Frome* produced?

How does *Ethan Frome* present its subject?

Who reads *Ethan Frome*? How do they interpret it?

Ethan Frome is presented complete and uninterrupted. You will find some words in the text asterisked: these are words which may be unfamiliar because they have a particular cultural or linguistic significance. They are explained in the Glossary section at the back.

The Resource Notes encourage you to take an active and imaginative approach to studying the novel both in and out of the classroom. As well as providing you with information about many aspects of *Ethan Frome*, they offer a wide choice of activities to work on individually, or in groups. Above all, they give you the chance to explore this heart-rending novel in a variety of ways: as a reader, an actor, a researcher, a critic, and a writer.

Judith Baxter

Ethan Frome

Edith Wharton

Edited by Robin Peel

Series Editor: Judith Baxter

With thanks to Jenny Lloyd for her contribution to this edition.

PUBLISHED BY THE PRESS SYNDICATE OF THE UNIVERSITY OF CAMBRIDGE
The Pitt Building, Trumpington Street, Cambridge CB2 1RP, United Kingdom

CAMBRIDGE UNIVERSITY PRESS
The Edinburgh Building, Cambridge CB2 2RU, United Kingdom
40 West 20th Street, New York, NY 10011-4211, USA
10 Stamford Road, Oakleigh, Melbourne 3166, Australia

This edition first published 1999

Printed in the United Kingdom at the University Press, Cambridge

Typeset in Sabon and Meta

A catalogue record for this book is available from the British Library

ISBN 0 521 64529 8 paperback

Prepared for publication by Stenton Associates

Acknowledgement
The original of the facsimile on page 169 is at The Yale Collection of
American Literature, Beinecke Rare Book and Manuscript Library, Yale
University.

INTRODUCTION

Confronting a mystery

Ethan Frome presents us with a mystery. Who is this strange man Ethan Frome, a man who seems to have a dreadful secret? What is his story?

As she explains in her Introduction (pp.13–15), Edith Wharton had thought carefully about how she should tell Ethan's story. Stories usually work towards an end, and a reader always wants to find out what happens next, or how something ends. She knew that this is what drives the reader on. People are eager to know how things will end in stories, perhaps because they know that they can never predict how things end in life. We don't know what is going to happen tomorrow, let alone next year.

◆ *Pre-reading activities*

1 Pair discussion

If you were in a second-hand bookshop and you saw to your amazement that you could buy your own biography – a book which tells the story of your life – which not only described what has happened to you, but also what is happening, and what is going to happen in the future, would you buy it?

If the answer is 'yes', be prepared to say why. If the answer is 'no' be prepared to say why. You could keep a record of your ideas and of this discussion in an *Ethan Frome* reading log.

2 Prediction

In *Ethan Frome*, the narrator (the storyteller) takes the reader (you) on a journey to the early years of Ethan's life. The narrator starts to wonder about this mysterious man as soon as he sees him. He wants to find about his past, about the 'smash-up' that happened to him and why he is prematurely old. Once the narrator takes the reader back into this past, the next big question for both is: 'what will happen to Ethan to turn him into the man that he now is, a man who looks "as if he was dead and in hell now"?'

When you come to read *Ethan Frome*, pause at the end of Chapter 5 and see if you can predict the outcome. Remind yourself to do this by placing a note in your reading log saying that when you reach page 76 of the story you need to record your prediction.

Three issues in *Ethan Frome*
The idea of 'remote' places

In her autobiography, *A Backward Glance* (1934), Edith Wharton makes a comparison between the remoteness of her New England mountain setting for *Ethan Frome* and the Yorkshire moors which Emily Brontë used as a setting for *Wuthering Heights*. The setting is not the only similarity. Each story is told by a narrator who:

- has arrived in a remote place (it seems remote to him);
- meets a mysterious man whose history is revealed as the story jumps back a generation to the days when this mysterious man was young.

✦ *Activity*

Someone who is visiting a city, town or community for the first time can be expected to view the people and places differently from someone who lives there all the time. People may not realise that their home town is regarded as small and remote, or big and dangerous, until they hear a comment from a stranger. Think about how others see the area in which you live, and how *you* see other places.

Begin by jotting down some notes in response to the following questions, and then show these notes to your partner. Then report your responses to another pair who have done the same.

- Where seems far away and cut off to you?
- Do you feel that you live in a place that is exciting, or would you like to live somewhere else?

- Are there advantages in living in a place that is hard for outsiders to reach? Are there disadvantages?
- What impressions would a visitor who did not know your home area receive when she or he first arrived? Would they be accurate impressions?
- Would a visitor and a local person be aware of the same things?

Keep a record in your reading log of what you have written and said, and what you have heard others say, during this, and all other activities.

Duty and pleasure

One of the characteristics of being a child is that you are always on the look-out for pleasure. Eating sweets, playing, holidays, birthdays – these are the good things about being a child. As a teenager the search for pleasure continues. Think of things that young people like doing best.

The idea of *duty* can sometimes be remote: a sense of duty is something that parents have, or that people have in their work. For example, teachers, nurses, bus-drivers all have a duty to care for others and to take care.

Sometimes children and teenagers have many responsibilities too. If you are the oldest child, you may have looked after younger brothers or sisters. Some children and teenagers have to look after one or both of their parents. If you belong to a church it may be that the importance of putting duty above pleasure is often stressed to you. In some cases duty clashes with pleasure. You may wish to go out to a club or party, but may be duty-bound to stay in.

But is it as simple as this? It may be that being dutiful can give pleasure. But this is not often the case, and not the argument of *Ethan Frome*. Nonetheless, Edith Wharton's tale is concerned with duty.

✦ *Activity*

By using the procedure of making individual notes, sharing these ideas with a partner and discussing your responses with another pair in a group, consider the following ethical questions – questions concerning what we consider to be right or wrong – about duty, pleasure and romance:

- If you have a boyfriend or a girlfriend at home, would it be wrong to have a romantic evening out with someone else you liked while you were away on holiday? Give reasons for your answer.
- If someone is married, is it wrong for them to have an affair? Give reasons for your answer.
- If you marry someone and he or she begins to suffer from a long illness, is it your duty to look after that person?
- If the answer to the above question is 'yes', should you give up any ideas of future romance and devote yourself to looking after the person you married?
- If parents look after children who are not grateful for being looked after, or adults care for relatives who seem unappreciative, does that mean that they have less of a duty to look after them?

Continue to keep a record of these responses in your reading log.

Loneliness and entrapment

When *Ethan Frome* was first reviewed, it was criticised for being so pessimistic – that is, its ending was considered rather gloomy.

Later critics have called it the most *American* of Edith Wharton's books.

These two comments may seem to be contradictory. When people think of the United States they often think of the 'American Dream' and of optimism. Most of those who emigrated from Europe to the United States did so because they wanted to escape poverty or oppression, and to make a better life. This was the 'American Dream' – to become successful, to achieve wonderful things however humble your beginnings.

On the other hand, if you consider the theme of loneliness to be the central theme of American literature, then, as the critic Carol Wershovan (1982) argues, Wharton's novels are a variation on this very American theme.

New England was settled by Europeans who experienced both the dream and the loneliness. Amongst the first European settlers to colonise America were the Puritans, who settled there in the seventeenth century. They dreamed of success and freedom, but unlike many of those who followed them in later centuries, a number believed strongly in *predestination* and *sin*. They experienced feelings of isolation and loneliness, surrounded by a sense of a threatening, godless wilderness.

Predestination was a Christian belief associated with Calvinism – named after its Swiss founder John Calvin (1509–1564) – and it meant that your chances of going to heaven or hell were predetermined, so that your future was out of your control. Although this didn't result in everyone behaving badly (why would this be?), it did create the rather gloomy acceptance that the bad things that happened were inevitable and part of God's punishment for the sinfulness of the human race.

Edith Wharton was not a Calvinist, but despite her professional success as a writer, she felt trapped in her personal life. This feeling of entrapment is associated with all the characters in *Ethan Frome*, but most obviously with Ethan himself. 'He was a prisoner for life' we learn on page 100. It was a phrase used often by Edith Wharton to describe her own position in life. Coincidently, the same phrase was used by James Joyce (1882–1941) of Little Chandler, the central character in 'A Little Cloud' in *Dubliners* (1914). In *Dubliners* it is Irish Catholicism that is responsible for the Dubliners' inability to escape, while in *Ethan Frome* it seems to be the influence of American Puritanism that entraps a New Englander such as Ethan.

✦ *Activity*

Feeling trapped

Now compare the present day with the time in which the story is set – nearly a hundred years ago. Singly, then in pairs, and finally in groups (as before), establish your response to the following questions about what it can mean to feel trapped.

Do you think that people who find themselves in the following situations could understandably feel that they have 'drawn the short straw' in life and that they are trapped? Explain your 'yes' or 'no'.

	Then (a hundred years ago)	Now
Living in a poor district		
Being born female		
Being born into an ethnic minority		

The record of this discussion should be another entry in your reading log.

Edith Wharton's Introduction

The following Introduction was published alongside *Ethan Frome* when it appeared in 1911. Edith Wharton considered it very important and was eager that it should be read *before* the tale.

✦ *Activity*

Group discussion

When did you read the Introduction? In this edition of *Ethan Frome* the Introduction has been placed before the main text, as Edith Wharton intended. Have you read it before reading the main narrative? Many people go straight to page one of a story and then go back to the Introduction later.

In pairs, discuss which of the following statements you most agree with:

- Edith Wharton wrote this piece as an introduction, and intended it to be placed, and read, before the tale. It should therefore be read as intended, first.
- An introduction takes on a more significant meaning when the text to which it refers has been read, so that it is preferable to read the introduction *after* the main text.
- A reading of a text is shaped by all previous readings, of similar and different texts. This can be demonstrated by reading the Introduction twice – once before and once after – noting the response in each case and noting the differences (if there are any) in these responses.

Author's Introduction

I had known something of New England village life long before I made my home in the same county as my imaginary Starkfield; though, during the years spent there, certain of its aspects became much more familiar to me.

Even before that final initiation, however, I had had an uneasy sense that the New England of fiction bore little – except a vague botanical and dialectical – resemblance to the harsh and beautiful land as I had seen it. Even the abundant enumeration of sweet-fern, asters and mountain-laurel, and the conscientious reproduction of the vernacular, left me with the feeling that the outcropping granite had in both cases been overlooked. I give the impression merely as a personal one; it accounts for 'Ethan Frome', and may, to some readers, in a measure justify it.

So much for the origin of the story; there is nothing else of interest to say of it, except as concerns its construction.

The problem before me, as I saw in the first flash, was this: I had to deal with a subject of which the dramatic climax, or rather the anti-climax, occurs a generation later than the first acts of the tragedy. This enforced lapse of time would seem to anyone persuaded – as I have always been – that every subject (in the novelist's sense of the term) implicitly *contains its own form and dimensions*, to mark Ethan Frome as the subject for a novel. But I never thought this for a moment, for I had felt, at the same time, that the theme of my tale was not one on which many variations could be played. It must be treated as starkly and summarily as life had always presented itself to my protagonists; any attempt to elaborate and complicate their sentiments would necessarily have falsified the whole. They were, in truth, these figures, my *granite outcroppings*; but half-emerged from the soil, and scarcely more articulate.

This incompatibility between subject and plan would perhaps have seemed to suggest that my 'situation' was after all one to be rejected. Every novelist has been visited by the insinuating wraiths of false 'good situations', siren-subjects luring his cockle-shell to the rocks; their voice is oftenest heard, and their mirage-sea beheld, as he traverses the waterless desert which awaits him halfway through whatever work is actually in hand. I knew well enough what song those siren sang, and had often tied myself to my dull job until they were out of hearing – perhaps carrying a lost masterpiece in their rainbow veils. But I had no such fear of them in the case of Ethan Frome. It was the first subject I had ever approached with full confidence in its value, for my own purpose, and a relative faith in my power to render at least a part of what I saw in it.

Every novelist, again, who 'intends upon' his art, has lit upon such subjects, and been fascinated by the difficulty of presenting them in the fullest relief, yet without an added ornament, or a trick of drapery or lighting. This was my task, if I were to tell the story of Ethan Frome; and my scheme of construction – which met with the immediate and unqualified disapproval of the few friends to whom I tentatively outlined it – I still think justified in the given case. It appears to me, indeed, that, while an air of artificiality is lent to a tale of complex and sophisticated people which the novelist causes to be guessed at and interpreted by any mere looker-on, there need be no such drawback if the looker-on is sophisticated, and the people he interprets are simple. If he is capable of seeing all around them, no violence is done to probability in allowing him to exercise this faculty; it is natural enough that he should act as the sympathizing intermediary between his rudimentary characters and the more complicated minds to whom he is trying to present them. But this is all self-evident, and needs explaining only to those who have never thought of fiction as an art of composition.

The real merit of my construction seems to me to lie in a minor detail. I had to find means to bring my tragedy, in a way at once natural and picture-making, to the knowledge of its narrator. I might have sat him down before a village gossip who would have poured out the whole affair to him in a breath, but in doing this I should have been false to two essential elements of my picture: first, the deep-rooted reticence and inarticulateness of the people I was trying to draw, and secondly the effect of 'roundness' (in the plastic sense) produced by letting their case be seen through eyes as different as those of Harmon Gow and Mrs Ned Hale. Each of my chroniclers contributes to the narrative *just so much as he or she is capable of understanding* of what, to them, is a complicated and mysterious case; and only the narrator of the tale has scope enough to see it all, to resolve it back into simplicity, and to put it in its rightful place among his larger categories.

I make no claim for originality in following a method of which 'La Grande Bretêche'◊ and 'The Ring and the Book'◊ had set me the magnificent example; my one merit is, perhaps, to have guessed that the proceeding there employed was also applicable to my small tale.

I have written this brief analysis – the first I have ever published of any of my books – because, as an author's introduction to his work, I can imagine nothing of any value to his readers except a statement as to why he decided to attempt the work in question, and why he selected one form rather than another for its embodiment. These primary aims, the only ones that can be explicitly stated, must, by the artist, be almost instinctively felt and acted upon before there can pass into his creation that imponderable something more which causes life to circulate in it, and preserves it for a little from decay.

Edith Wharton

Ethan Frome

I had the story, bit by bit, from various people, and, as generally happens in such cases, each time it was a different story.

If you know Starkfield, Massachusetts, you know the post-office. If you know the post-office you must have seen Ethan Frome drive up to it, drop the reins on his hollow-backed bay° and drag himself across the brick pavement to the white colonnade: and you must have asked who he was.

It was there that, several years ago, I saw him for the first time; and the sight pulled me up sharp. Even then he was the most striking figure in Starkfield, though he was but the ruin of a man. It was not so much his great height that marked him, for the 'natives' were easily singled out by their lank longitude from the stockier foreign breed: it was the careless powerful look he had, in spite of a lameness checking each step like the jerk of a chain. There was something bleak and unapproachable in his face, and he was so stiffened and grizzled that I took him for an old man and was surprised to hear that he was not more than fifty-two. I had this from Harmon Gow, who had driven the stage from Bettsbridge to Starkfield in pre-trolley° days and knew the chronicle of all the families on his line.

'He's looked that way ever since he had his smash-up; and that's twenty-four years ago come next February,' Harmon threw out between reminiscent pauses.

The 'smash-up' it was – I gathered from the same informant – which, besides drawing the red gash across Ethan Frome's forehead, had so shortened and warped his right side that it cost him a visible effort to take the few steps from his buggy to the post-office window. He used to drive in from his farm every day at about noon, and as that was my own hour for fetching my mail I often passed him in the porch or stood beside him while we waited on the motions of the distributing hand behind the grating. I noticed that, though he came so punctually, he seldom received anything but a copy of the *Bettsbridge Eagle*, which he put without a glance into his sagging pocket. At intervals, however, the post-master would hand him an envelope addressed to Mrs Zenobia – or Mrs Zeena – Frome, and usually bearing conspicuously in the upper left-hand corner the address of some manufacturer of patent medicine and the name of his specific. These documents my neighbour would also pocket without a glance, as if too much used to them to wonder at their number and variety, and would then turn away with a silent nod to the post-master.

Every one in Starkfield knew him and gave him a greeting tempered to his own grave mien; but his taciturnity was respected and it was only on rare occasions that one of the older men of the place detained him for a word. When this happened he would listen quietly, his blue eyes on the speaker's face, and answer in so low a tone that his words never reached me; then he would climb stiffly into his buggy, gather up the reins in his left hand and drive slowly away in the direction of his farm.

'It was a pretty bad smash-up?' I questioned Harmon, looking after Frome's retreating figure, and thinking how gallantly his lean brown head, with its shock of light hair, must have sat on his strong shoulders before they were bent out of shape.

'Wust kind,' my informant assented. 'More'n enough to kill most men. But the Fromes are tough. Ethan'll likely touch a hundred.'

'Good God!' I exclaimed. At the moment Ethan Frome, after climbing to his seat, had leaned over to assure himself of the security of a wooden box – also with a druggist's label on it – which he had placed in the back of the buggy, and I saw his face as it probably looked when he thought himself alone.

'*That* man touch a hundred? He looks as if he was dead and in hell now!'

Harmon drew a slab of tobacco from his pocket, cut off a wedge and pressed it into the leather pouch of his cheek. 'Guess he's been in Starkfield too many winters. Most of the smart ones get away.'

'Why didn't *he*?'

'Somebody had to stay and care for the folks. There warn't ever anybody but Ethan. Fust his father – then his mother – then his wife.'

'And then the smash-up?'

Harmon chuckled sardonically. 'That's so. He *had* to stay then.'

'I see. And since then they've had to care for him?'

Harmon thoughtfully passed his tobacco to the other cheek. 'Oh, as to that: I guess it's always Ethan done the caring.'

Though Harmon Gow developed the tale as far as his mental and moral reach permitted there were perceptible gaps between his facts, and I had the sense that the deeper meaning of the story was in the gaps. But one phrase stuck in my memory and served as the nucleus about which I grouped my subsequent inferences: 'Guess he's been in Starkfield too many winters.'

Before my own time there was up I had learned to know what that meant. Yet I had come in the degenerate day of trolley, bicycle and rural delivery, when communication was easy between the scattered mountain villages, and the bigger towns in the valleys, such as Bettsbridge and Shadd's Falls, had libraries, theatres and Y. M. C. A. halls to which the youth of the hills could descent for recreation. But when winter shut down on Starkfield, and the village lay under a sheet of snow perpetually renewed from the pale skies, I began to see what life there – or rather its negation – must have been in Ethan Frome's young manhood.

I had been sent up by my employers on a job connected with the big power-house° at Corbury Junction, and a long-drawn carpenters' strike had so delayed the work that I found myself anchored at Starkfield – the nearest habitable spot – for the best part of the winter. I chafed at first, and then, under the hypnotising effect of routine, gradually began to find a grim satisfaction in the life. During the early part of my stay I had been struck by the contrast between the vitality of the climate and the deadness of the community. Day by day, after the December snows were over, a blazing blue sky poured down torrents of light and air on the white landscape, which gave them back in an intenser glitter. One would have supposed that such an atmosphere must quicken the emotions as well as the blood; but it seemed to produce no change except that of retarding still more the sluggish pulse of Starkfield. When I had been there a little longer, and had seen this phase of crystal clearness followed by long stretches of sunless cold; when the storms of February had pitched their white tents about the devoted village and the wild cavalry of March winds had charged down to their support; I began to understand why Starkfield emerged from its six months' siege like a starved garrison capitulating without quarter. Twenty years earlier the means of resistance must have been far fewer, and the enemy in command of almost all the lines of access between the beleaguered villages; and, considering these things, I felt the sinister force of Harmon's phrase: 'Most of the smart ones get away.' But if that were the case, how could any combination of obstacles have hindered the flight of a man like Ethan Frome?

During my stay at Starkfield I lodged with a middle-aged widow colloquially known as Mrs Ned Hale. Mrs Hale's father had been the village lawyer of the previous generation, and 'lawyer Varnum's house', where my landlady still lived with her mother, was the most considerable mansion in the village. It stood at one end of the main street, its classic portico and small-paned windows looking down a flagged path between Norway spruces to the slim white steeple of the Congregational church. It was clear that the Varnum fortunes were at the ebb, but the two women did what they could to preserve a decent dignity; and Mrs Hale, in particular, had a certain wan refinement not out of keeping with her pale old-fashioned house.

In the 'best parlour', with its black horse-hair and mahogany weakly illuminated by a gurgling Carcel lamp,◇ I listened every evening to another and more delicately shaded version of the Starkfield chronicle. It was not that Mrs Ned Hale felt, or affected, any social superiority to the people about her; it was only that the accident of a finer sensibility and a little more education had put just enough distance between herself and her neighbours to enable her to judge them with detachment. She was not unwilling to exercise this faculty, and I had great hopes of getting from her the missing facts of Ethan Frome's story, or rather such a key to his character as should co-ordinate the facts I knew. Her mind was a store-house of innocuous anecdote and any question about her acquaintances brought forth a volume of detail; but on the subject of Ethan Frome I found her unexpectedly reticent. There was no hint of disapproval in her reserve; I merely felt in her an insurmountable reluctance to speak of him or his affairs, a low 'Yes, I knew them both ... it was awful ...' seeming to be the utmost concession that her distress could make to my curiosity.

So marked was the change in her manner, such depths of sad initiation did it imply, that, with some doubts as to my delicacy, I put the case anew to my village oracle, Harmon Gow; but got for my pains only an uncomprehending grunt.

'Ruth Varnum was always as nervous as a rat; and, come to think of it, she was the first one to see 'em after they was picked up. It happened right below lawyer Varnum's, down at the bend of the Corbury road, just round about the time that

Ruth got engaged to Ned Hale. The young folks was all friends, and I guess she just can't bear to talk about it. She's had troubles enough of her own.'

All the dwellers in Starkfield, as in more notable communities, had had troubles enough of their own to make them comparatively indifferent to those of their neighbours; and though all conceded that Ethan Frome's had been beyond the common measure, no one gave me an explanation of the look in his face which, as I persisted in thinking, neither poverty nor physical suffering could have put there. Nevertheless, I might have contented myself with the story pieced together from these hints had it not been for the provocation of Mrs Hale's silence, and – a little later – for the accident of personal contact with the man.

On my arrival at Starkfield, Denis Eady, the rich Irish grocer, who was the proprietor of Starkfield's nearest approach to a livery stable, had entered into an agreement to send me over daily to Corbury Flats, where I had to pick up my train for the Junction. But about the middle of the winter Eady's horses fell ill of a local epidemic. The illness spread to the other Starkfield stables and for a day or two I was put to it to find a means of transport. Then Harmon Gow suggested that Ethan Frome's bay was still on his legs and that his owner might be glad to drive me over.

I stared at the suggestion. 'Ethan Frome? But I've never even spoken to him. Why on earth should he put himself out for me?'

Harmon's answer surprised me still more. 'I don't know as he would; but I know he wouldn't be sorry to earn a dollar.'

I had been told that Frome was poor, and that the saw-mill and the arid acres of his farm yielded scarcely enough to keep his household through the winter; but I had not supposed him to be in such want as Harmon's words implied, and I expressed my wonder.

'Well, matters ain't gone any too well with him,' Harmon said. 'When a man's been setting round like a hulk for twenty years or more, seeing things that want doing, it eats inter him, and he loses his grit. That Frome farm was always 'bout as bare's a milkpan when the cat's been round; and you know what one of them old water-mills is wuth nowadays. When Ethan could sweat over 'em both from sun-up to dark he kinder choked a living out of 'em; but his folks ate up most everything, even then, and I don't see how he makes out now. Fust his father got a kick, out haying, and went soft in the brain, and gave away money like Bible texts afore he died. Then his mother got queer and dragged along for years as weak as a baby; and his wife Zeena, she's always been the greatest hand at doctoring in the county. Sickness and trouble: that's what Ethan's had his plate full up with, ever since the very first helping.'

The next morning, when I looked out, I saw the hollow-backed bay between the Varnum spruces, and Ethan Frome, throwing back his worn bearskin, made room for me in the sleigh at his side. After that, for a week, he drove me over every morning to Corbury Flats, and on my return in the afternoon met me again and carried me back through the icy night to Starkfield. The distance each way was barely three miles, but the old bay's pace was slow, and even with firm snow under the runners we were nearly an hour on the way. Ethan Frome drove in silence, the reins loosely held in his left hand, his brown seamed profile, under the helmet-like peak of the cap, relieved against the banks of snow like the bronze image of a hero. He never turned his face to mine, or answered, except in monosyllables, the questions I put, or such slight pleasantries as I ventured. He seemed a part of the mute melancholy landscape, an incarnation of its frozen woe, with all that was warm and sentient in him fast bound below the surface; but there was nothing unfriendly in his silence. I simply felt that he lived in a depth of moral isolation too remote for casual access, and I had the sense that his loneliness was not merely the result of his personal plight, tragic as I guessed that to be, but had in it, as Harmon Gow had hinted, the profound accumulated cold of many Starkfield winters.

Only once or twice was the distance between us bridged for a moment; and the glimpses thus gained confirmed my desire to know more. Once I happened to speak of an engineering job I had been on the previous year in Florida, and of the contrast between the winter landscape about us and that in which I had found myself the year before; and to my surprise Frome said suddenly: 'Yes: I was down there once, and for a good while afterward I could call up the sight of it in winter. But now it's all snowed under.'

He said no more, and I had to guess the rest from the inflection of his voice and his sharp relapse into silence.

Another day, on getting into my train at the Flats, I missed a volume of popular science – I think it was on some recent discoveries in biochemistry – which I had carried with me to read on the way. I thought no more about it till I got into the sleigh again that evening, and saw the book in Frome's hand.

'I found it after you were gone,' he said.

I put the volume into my pocket and we dropped back into our usual silence; but as we began to crawl up the long hill from Corbury Flats to the Starkfield ridge I became aware in the dusk that he had turned his face to mine.

'There are things in that book that I didn't know the first word about,' he said.

I wondered less at his words than at the queer note of resentment in his voice. He was evidently surprised and slightly aggrieved at his own ignorance.

'Does that sort of thing interest you?' I asked.

'It used to.'

'There are one or two rather new things in the book: there have been some big strides lately in that particular line of research.' I waited a moment for an answer that did not come;

then I said: 'If you'd like to look the book through I'd be glad to leave it with you.'

He hesitated, and I had the impression that he felt himself about to yield to a stealing tide of inertia; then, 'Thank you – I'll take it,' he answered shortly.

I hoped that this incident might set up some more direct communication between us. Frome was so simple and straightforward that I was sure his curiosity about the book was based on a genuine interest in its subject. Such tastes and acquirements in a man of his condition made the contrast more poignant between his outer situation and his inner needs, and I hoped that the chance of giving expression to the latter might at least unseal his lips. But something in his past history, or in his present way of living, had apparently driven him too deeply into himself for any casual impulse to draw him back to his kind. At our next meeting he made no allusion to the book, and our intercourse seemed fated to remain as negative and one-sided as if there had been no break in his reserve.

Frome had been driving me over to the Flats for about a week when one morning I looked out of my window into a thick snow-fall. The height of the white waves massed against the garden-fence and along the wall of the church showed that the storm must have been going on all night, and that the drifts were likely to be heavy in the open. I thought it probable that my train would be delayed; but I had to be at the power-house for an hour or two that afternoon, and I decided, if Frome turned up, to push through to the Flats and wait there till my train came in. I don't know why I put it in the conditional, however, for I never doubted that Frome would appear. He was not the kind of man to be turned from his business by any commotion of the elements; and at the appointed hour his sleigh glided up through the snow like a stage-apparition behind thickening veils of gauze.

I was getting to know him too well to express either wonder or gratitude at his keeping his appointment; but I exclaimed in surprise as I saw him turn his horse in a direction opposite to that of the Corbury road.

'The railroad's blocked by a freight-train that got stuck in a drift below the Flats,' he explained, as we jogged off into the stinging whiteness.

'But look here – where are you taking me, then?'

'Straight to the Junction, by the shortest way,' he answered, pointing up School House Hill with his whip.

'To the Junction – in this storm? Why, it's a good ten miles!'

'The bay'll do it if you give him time. You said you had some business there this afternoon. I'll see you get there.'

He said it so quietly that I could only answer: 'You're doing me the biggest kind of a favour.'

'That's all right,' he rejoined.

Abreast of the schoolhouse the road forked, and we dipped down a lane to the left, between hemlock boughs bent inward to their trunks by the weight of the snow. I had often walked that way on Sundays, and knew that the solitary roof showing through bare branches near the bottom of the hill was that of Frome's saw-mill. It looked exanimate enough, with its idle wheel looming above the black stream dashed with yellow-white spume, and its cluster of sheds sagging under their white load. Frome did not even turn his head as we drove by, and still in silence we began to mount the next slope. About a mile farther, on a road I had never travelled, we came to an orchard of starved apple-trees writhing over a hillside among outcroppings of slate that nuzzled up through the snow like animals pushing out their noses to breathe. Beyond the orchard lay a field or two, their boundaries lost under drifts; and above the fields, huddled against the white immensities of land and sky, one of those lonely New England farm-houses that make the landscape lonelier.

'That's my place,' said Frome, with a sideway jerk of his lame elbow; and in the distress and oppression of the scene I did not know what to answer. The snow had ceased, and a flash of watery sunlight exposed the house on the slope above us in all its plaintive ugliness. The black wraith of a deciduous creeper flapped from the porch, and the thin wooden walls, under their worn coat of paint, seemed to shiver in the wind that had risen with the ceasing of the snow.

'The house was bigger in my father's time: I had to take down the 'L', a while back,' Frome continued, checking with a twitch of the left rein the bay's evident intention of turning in through the broken-down gate.

I saw then that the unusually forlorn and stunted look of the house was partly due to the loss of what is known in New England as the 'L': that long deep-roofed adjunct usually built at right angles to the main house, and connecting it, by way of storerooms and tool-house, with the wood-shed and cowbarn. Whether because of its symbolic sense, the image it presents of a life linked with the soil, and enclosing in itself the chief sources of warmth and nourishment, or whether merely because of the consolatory thought that it enables the dwellers in that harsh climate to get to their morning's work without facing the weather, it is certain that the 'L' rather than the house itself seems to be the centre, the actual hearth-stone of the New England farm. Perhaps this connection of ideas, which had often occurred to me in my rambles about Starkfield, caused me to hear a wistful note in Frome's words, and to see in the diminished dwelling the image of his own shrunken body.

'We're kinder side-tracked here now,' he added, 'but there was considerable passing before the railroad was carried through to the Flats.' He roused the lagging bay with another twitch; then, as if the mere sight of the house had let me too deeply into his confidence for any farther pretence of reserve, he went on slowly: 'I've always set down the worst of mother's trouble to that. When she got the rheumatism so bad she couldn't move around she used to sit up there and watch the road by the hour; and one year, when they was six months mending the Bettsbridge pike after the floods, and Harmon Gow had to bring his stage round this way, she picked up so that she used to get down to the gate most days to see him. But after the trains begun running nobody ever come by here to speak of, and mother never could get it through her head what had happened, and it preyed on her right along till she died.'

As we turned into the Corbury road the snow began to fall again, cutting off our last glimpse of the house; and Frome's silence fell with it, letting down between us the old veil of reticence. This time the wind did not cease with the return of the snow. Instead, it sprang up to a gale which now and then, from a tattered sky, flung pale sweeps of sunlight over a landscape chaotically tossed. But the bay was as good as Frome's word, and we pushed on to the Junction through the wild white scene.

In the afternoon the storm held off, and the clearness in the west seemed to my inexperienced eye the pledge of a fair evening. I finished my business as quickly as possible, and we set out for Starkfield with a good chance of getting there for supper. But at sunset the clouds gathered again, bringing an earlier night, and the snow began to fall straight and steadily from a sky without wind, in a soft universal diffusion more confusing than the gusts and eddies of the morning. It seemed to be a part of the thickening darkness, to be the winter night itself descending on us layer by layer.

The small ray of Frome's lantern was soon lost in this smothering medium, in which even his sense of direction, and the bay's homing instinct, finally ceased to serve us. Two or three times some ghostly landmark sprang up to warn us that we were astray, and then was sucked back into the mist; and when we finally regained our road the old horse began to show signs of exhaustion. I felt myself to blame for having accepted Frome's offer, and after a short discussion I persuaded him to let me get out of the sleigh and walk along through the snow at the bay's side. In this way we struggled on for another mile or two, and at last reached a point where Frome, peering into what seemed to me formless night, said: 'That's my gate down yonder.'

The last stretch had been the hardest part of the way. The bitter cold and the heavy going had nearly knocked the wind out of me, and I could feel the horse's side ticking like a clock under my hand.

'Look here, Frome,' I began, 'there's no earthly use in your going any farther – ' but he interrupted me: 'Nor you neither. There's been about enough of this for anybody.'

I understood that he was offering me a night's shelter at the farm, and without answering I turned into the gate at his side, and followed him to the barn, where I helped him to unharness and bed down the tired horse. When this was done he unhooked the lantern from the sleigh, stepped out again into the night, and called to me over his shoulder: 'This way.'

Far off above us a square of light trembled through the screen of snow. Staggering along in Frome's wake I floundered toward it, and in the darkness almost fell into one of the deep drifts against the front of the house. Frome scrambled up the slippery steps of the porch, digging a way through the snow with his heavily booted foot. Then he lifted his lantern, found the latch, and led the way into the house. I went after him into a low unlit passage, at the back of which a ladder-like staircase rose into obscurity. On our right a line of light marked the door of the room which had sent its ray across the night; and behind the door I heard a woman's voice droning querulously.

Frome stamped on the worn oil-cloth to shake the snow from his boots, and set down his lantern on a kitchen chair which was the only piece of furniture in the hall. Then he opened the door.

'Come in,' he said; and as he spoke the droning voice grew still ...

It was that night that I found the clue to Ethan Frome, and began to put together this vision of his story ... ...

Chapter 1

The village lay under two feet of snow, with drifts at the windy corners. In a sky of iron the points of the Dipper hung like icicles and Orion° flashed his cold fires. The moon had set, but the night was so transparent that the white house-fronts between the elms looked grey against the snow, clumps of bushes made black stains on it, and the basement windows of the church sent shafts of yellow light far across the endless undulations.

Young Ethan Frome walked at a quick pace along the deserted street, past the bank and Michael Eady's new brick store and lawyer Varnum's house with the two black Norway spruces at the gate. Opposite the Varnum gate, where the road fell away toward the Corbury valley, the church reared its slim white steeple and narrow peristyle. As the young man walked toward it the upper windows drew a black arcade along the side wall of the building, but from the lower openings, on the side where the ground sloped steeply down to the Corbury road, the light shot its long bars, illuminating many fresh furrows in the track leading to the basement door, and showing, under an adjoining shed, a line of sleighs with heavily blanketed horses.

The night was perfectly still, and the air so dry and pure that it gave little sensation of cold. The effect produced on Frome was rather of a complete absence of atmosphere, as though nothing less tenuous than ether intervened between the white earth under his feet and the metallic dome overhead. 'It's like being in an exhausted receiver,' he thought. Four or five years earlier he had taken a year's course at a technological college at Worcester, and dabbled in the laboratory with a friendly professor of physics; and the images supplied by that experience still cropped up, at unexpected moments, through the totally different associations of thought in which he had since been living. His father's death, and the misfortunes following it, had put a premature end to Ethan's studies; but though they had not gone far enough to be of much practical use they had fed his fancy and made him aware of huge cloudy meanings behind the daily face of things.

As he strode along through the snow the sense of such meanings glowed in his brain and mingled with the bodily flush produced by his sharp tramp. At the end of the village he paused before the darkened front of the church. He stood there a moment, breathing quickly, and looking up and down the street, in which not another figure moved. The pitch of the Corbury road, below lawyer Varnum's spruces, was the favourite coasting-ground of Starkfield, and on clear evenings the church corner rang till late with the shouts of the coasters; but to-night not a sled darkened the whiteness of the long declivity. The hush of midnight lay on the village, and all its waking life was gathered behind the church windows, from which strains of dance-music flowed with the broad bands of yellow light.

The young man, skirting the side of the building, went down the slope toward the basement door. To keep out of range of the revealing rays from within he made a circuit through the untrodden snow and gradually approached the farther angle of the basement wall. Thence, still hugging the shadow, he edged his way cautiously forward to the nearest window, holding back his straight spare body and craning his neck till he got a glimpse of the room.

Seen thus, from the pure and frosty darkness in which he stood, it seemed to be seething in a mist of heat. The metal reflectors of the gas-jets sent crude waves of light against the whitewashed walls, and the iron flanks of the stove at the end of the hall looked as though they were heaving with volcanic fires. The floor was thronged with girls and young men. Down the side wall facing the window stood a row of kitchen chairs from which the older women had just risen. By this time the music had stopped, and the musicians – a fiddler, and the young lady who played the harmonium on Sundays – were hastily refreshing themselves at one corner of the supper-table which aligned its devastated pie-dishes and ice-cream saucers on the platform at the end of the hall. The guests were preparing to leave, and the tide had already set toward the passage where coats and wraps were hung, when a young man with a sprightly foot and a shock of black hair shot into the middle of the floor and clapped his hands. The signal took instant effect. The musicians hurried to their instruments, the dancers – some already half-muffled for departure – fell into line down each side of the room, the older spectators slipped back to their chairs, and the lively young man, after diving about here and there in the throng, drew forth a girl who had already wound a cherry-coloured 'fascinator'* about her head, and, leading her up to the end of the floor, whirled her down its length to the bounding tune of a Virginia reel.*

Frome's heart was beating fast. He had been straining for a glimpse of the dark head under the cherry-coloured scarf and it vexed him that another eye should have been quicker than his. The leader of the reel, who looked as if he had Irish blood in his veins, danced well, and his partner caught his fire. As she passed down the line, her light figure swinging from hand to hand in circles of increasing swiftness, the scarf flew off her head and stood out behind her shoulders, and Frome, at each turn, caught sight of her laughing panting lips, the cloud of dark hair about her forehead, and the dark eyes which seemed the only fixed points in a maze of flying lines.

The dancers were going faster and faster, and the musicians, to keep up with them, belaboured their instruments like jockeys lashing their mounts on the home-stretch; yet it seemed to the young man at the window that the reel would never end. Now and then he turned his eyes from the girl's face to that of her partner, which, in the exhilaration of the dance, had taken on a look of almost impudent ownership. Denis Eady was the son of Michael Eady, the ambitious Irish grocer, whose suppleness and effrontery had given Starkfield its first notion of 'smart' business methods, and whose new brick store testified to the success of the attempt. His son seemed likely to follow in his steps, and was meanwhile applying the same arts to the conquest of the Starkfield maidenhood. Hitherto Ethan Frome had been content to think him a mean fellow; but now he positively invited a horse-whipping. It was strange that the girl did not seem aware of it: that she could lift her rapt face to her dancer's, and drop her hands into his, without appearing to feel the offence of his look and touch.

Frome was in the habit of walking into Starkfield to fetch home his wife's cousin, Mattie Silver, on the rare evenings when some chance of amusement drew her to the village. It was his wife who had suggested, when the girl came to live with them, that such opportunities should be put in her way. Mattie Silver came from Stamford, and when she entered the Fromes' household to act as her cousin Zeena's aid it was thought best, as she came without pay, not to let her feel too sharp a contrast between the life she had left and the isolation of a Starkfield farm. But for this – as Frome sardonically reflected – it would hardly have occurred to Zeena to take any thought for the girl's amusement.

When his wife first proposed that they should give Mattie an occasional evening out he had inwardly demurred at having to do the extra two miles to the village and back after his hard day on the farm; but not long afterward he had reached the point of wishing that Starkfield might give all its nights to revelry.

Mattie Silver had lived under his roof for a year, and from early morning till they met at supper he had frequent chances of seeing her; but no moments in her company were comparable to those when, her arm in his, and her light step flying to keep time with his long stride, they walked back through the night to the farm. He had taken to the girl from the first day, when he had driven over to the Flats to meet her, and she had smiled and waved to him from the train, crying out, 'You must be Ethan!' as she jumped down with her bundles, while he reflected, looking over her slight person: 'She don't look much on housework, but she ain't a fretter, anyhow.' But it was not only that the coming to his house of a bit of hopeful young life was like the lighting of a fire on a cold hearth. The girl was more than the bright serviceable creature he had thought her. She had an eye to see and an ear to hear: he could show her things and tell her things, and taste the bliss of feeling that all he imparted left long reverberations and echoes he could wake at will.

It was during their night walks back to the farm that he felt most intensely the sweetness of this communion. He had always been more sensitive than the people about him to the appeal of natural beauty. His unfinished studies had given form to this sensibility and even in his unhappiest moments field and sky spoke to him with a deep and powerful persuasion. But hitherto the emotion had remained in him as a silent ache, veiling with sadness the beauty that evoked it. He did not even know whether any one else in the world felt as he did, or whether he was the sole victim of this mournful privilege. Then he learned that one other spirit had trembled with the same touch of wonder: that at his side, living under his roof and eating his bread, was a creature to whom he could say: 'That's Orion down yonder; the big fellow to the right is Aldebaran, and the bunch of little ones – like bees swarming – they're the Pleiades ...'* or whom he could hold entranced before a ledge of granite thrusting up through the fern while he unrolled the huge panorama of the ice age, and the long dim stretches of succeeding time. The fact that admiration for his learning mingled with Mattie's wonder at what he taught was not the least part of his pleasure. And there were other sensations, less definable but more exquisite, which drew them together with a shock of silent joy: the cold red of sunset behind winter hills, the flight of cloud-flocks over slopes of golden stubble, or the intensely blue shadows of hemlocks on sunlit snow. When she said to him once: 'It looks just as if it was painted!' it seemed to Ethan that the art of definition could go no farther, and that words had at last been found to utter his secret soul ...

As he stood in the darkness outside the church these memories came back with the poignancy of vanished things. Watching Mattie whirl down the floor from hand to hand he wondered how he could ever have thought that his dull talk interested her. To him, who was never gay but in her presence, her gaiety seemed plain proof of indifference. The face she lifted to her dancers was the same which, when she saw him, always looked like a window that has caught the sunset. He even noticed two or three gestures which, in his fatuity, he had thought she kept for him: a way of throwing her head back when she was amused, as if to taste her laugh before she let it out, and a trick of sinking her lids slowly when anything charmed or moved her.

The sight made him unhappy, and his unhappiness roused his latent fears. His wife had never shown any jealousy of Mattie, but of late she had grumbled increasingly over the house-work and found oblique ways of attracting attention to the girl's inefficiency. Zeena had always been what Starkfield called 'sickly', and Frome had to admit that, if she were as ailing as she believed, she needed the help of a stronger arm than the one which lay so lightly in his during the night walks to the farm. Mattie had no natural turn for house-keeping, and her training had done nothing to remedy the defect. She was quick to learn, but forgetful and dreamy, and not disposed to take the matter seriously. Ethan had an idea that if she were to marry a man she was fond of the dormant instinct would wake, and her pies and biscuits become the pride of the county; but domesticity in the abstract did not interest her. At first she was so awkward that he could not help laughing at her; but she laughed with him and that made them better friends. He did his best to supplement her unskilled efforts, getting up earlier than usual to light the kitchen fire, carrying in the wood overnight, and neglecting the mill for the farm that he might help her about the house during the day. He even crept down on Saturday nights to scrub the kitchen floor after the women had gone to bed; and Zeena, one day, had surprised him at the churn and had turned away silently, with one of her queer looks.

Of late there had been other signs of her disfavour, as intangible but more disquieting. One cold winter morning, as he dressed in the dark, his candle flickering in the draught of the ill-fitting window, he had heard her speak from the bed behind him.

'The doctor don't want I should be left without anybody to do for me,' she said in her flat whine.

He had supposed her to be asleep, and the sound of her voice had startled him, though she was given to abrupt explosions of speech after long intervals of secretive silence.

He turned and looked at her where she lay indistinctly outlined under the dark calico quilt, her high-boned face taking a greyish tinge from the whiteness of the pillow.

'Nobody to do for you?' he repeated.

'If you say you can't afford a hired girl when Mattie goes.'

Frome turned away again, and taking up his razor stooped to catch the reflection of his stretched cheek in the blotched looking-glass above the wash-stand.

'Why on earth should Mattie go?'

'Well, when she gets married, I mean,' his wife's drawl came from behind him.

'Oh, she'd never leave us as long as you needed her,' he returned, scraping hard at his chin.

'I wouldn't ever have it said that I stood in the way of a poor girl like Mattie marrying a smart fellow like Denis Eady,' Zeena answered in a tone of plaintive self-effacement.

Ethan, glaring at his face in the glass, threw his head back to draw the razor from ear to chin. His hand was steady, but the attitude was an excuse for not making an immediate reply.

'And the doctor don't want I should be left without anybody,' Zeena continued. 'He wanted I should speak to you about a girl he's heard about, that might come — '

Ethan laid down the razor and straightened himself with a laugh.

'Denis Eady! If that's all, I guess there's no such hurry to look round for a girl.'

'Well, I'd like to talk to you about it,' said Zeena obstinately.

He was getting into his clothes in fumbling haste. 'All right. But I haven't got the time now; I'm late as it is,' he returned, holding his old silver turnip-watch* to the candle.

Zeena, apparently accepting this as final, lay watching him in silence while he pulled his suspenders over his shoulders and jerked his arms into his coat; but as he went toward the door she said, suddenly and incisively: 'I guess you're always late, now you shave every morning.'

That thrust had frightened him more than any vague insinuations about Denis Eady. It was a fact that since Mattie Silver's coming he had taken to shaving every day; but his wife always seemed to be asleep when he left her side in the winter darkness, and he had stupidly assumed that she would not notice any change in his appearance. Once or twice in the past he had been faintly disquieted by Zenobia's way of letting things happen without seeming to remark them, and then, weeks afterward, in a casual phrase, revealing that she had all along taken her notes and drawn her inferences. Of late, however, there had been no room in his thoughts for such vague apprehensions. Zeena herself, from an oppressive reality, had faded into an insubstantial shade. All his life was lived in the sight and sound of Mattie Silver, and he could no longer conceive of its being otherwise. But now, as he stood outside the church, and saw Mattie spinning down the floor with Denis Eady, a throng of disregarded hints and menaces wove their cloud about his brain …

Chapter 2

As the dancers poured out of the hall Frome, drawing back behind the projecting storm-door, watched the segregation of the grotesquely muffled groups, in which a moving lantern ray now and then lit up a face flushed with food and dancing. The villagers, being afoot, were the first to climb the slope to the main street, while the country neighbours packed themselves more slowly into the sleighs under the shed.

'Ain't you riding, Mattie?' a woman's voice called back from the throng about the shed, and Ethan's heart gave a jump. From where he stood he could not see the persons coming out of the hall till they had advanced a few steps beyond the wooden sides of the storm-door; but through its cracks he heard a clear voice answer: 'Mercy no! Not on such a night.'

She was there, then, close to him, only a thin board between. In another moment she would step forth into the night, and his eyes, accustomed to the obscurity, would discern her as clearly as though she stood in daylight. A wave of shyness pulled him back into the dark angle of the wall, and he stood there in silence instead of making his presence known to her. It had been one of the wonders of their intercourse that from the first, she, the quicker, finer, more expressive, instead of crushing him by the contrast, had given him something of her own ease and freedom; but now he felt as heavy and loutish as in his student days, when he had tried to 'jolly' the Worcester girls at a picnic.

He hung back, and she came out alone and paused within a few yards of him. She was almost the last to leave the hall, and she stood looking uncertainly about her as if wondering why he did not show himself. Then a man's figure approached, coming so close to her that under their formless wrappings they seemed merged in one dim outline.

'Gentleman friend gone back on you? Say, Matt, that's tough! No, I wouldn't be mean enough to tell the other girls. I ain't as low-down as that.' (How Frome hated his cheap banter!) 'But look a here, ain't it lucky I got the old man's cutter◦ down there waiting for us?'

Frome heard the girl's voice, gaily incredulous: 'What on earth's your father's cutter doin' down there?'

'Why, waiting for me to take a ride. I got the roan colt◦ too. I kinder knew I'd want to take a ride to-night,' Eady, in his triumph, tried to put a sentimental note into his bragging voice.

The girl seemed to waver, and Frome saw her twirl the end of her scarf irresolutely about her fingers. Not for the world would he have made a sign to her, though it seemed to him that his life hung on her next gesture.

'Hold on a minute while I unhitch the colt,' Denis called to her, springing toward the shed.

She stood perfectly still, looking after him, in an attitude of tranquil expectancy torturing to the hidden watcher. Frome noticed that she no longer turned her head from side to side, as though peering through the night for another figure. She let Denis Eady lead out the horse, climb into the cutter and fling back the bearskin to make room for her at his side; then, with a swift motion of flight, she turned about and darted up the slope toward the front of the church.

'Good-bye! Hope you'll have a lovely ride!' she called back to him over her shoulder.

Denis laughed, and gave the horse a cut that brought him quickly abreast of her retreating figure.

'Come along! Get in quick! It's as slippery as thunder on this turn,' he cried, leaning over to reach out a hand to her.

She laughed back at him: 'Good-night! I'm not getting in.'

By this time they had passed beyond Frome's earshot and he could only follow the shadowy pantomime of their silhouettes as they continued to move along the crest of the slope above him. He saw Eady, after a moment, jump from the cutter and go toward the girl with the reins over one arm. The other he tried to slip through hers; but she eluded him nimbly, and Frome's heart, which had swung out over a black void, trembled back to safety. A moment later he heard the jingle of departing sleigh-bells and discerned a figure advancing along toward the empty expanse of snow before the church.

In the black shade of the Varnum spruces he caught up with her and she turned with a quick 'Oh!'

'Think I'd forgotten you, Matt?' he asked with sheepish glee.

She answered seriously: 'I thought maybe you couldn't come back for me.'

'Couldn't? What on earth could stop me?'

'I knew Zeena wasn't feeling any too good to-day.'

'Oh, she's in bed long ago.' He paused, a question struggling in him. 'Then you meant to walk home all alone?'

'Oh, I ain't afraid!' she laughed.

They stood together in the gloom of the spruces, an empty world glimmering about them wide and grey under the stars. He brought his question out.

'If you thought I hadn't come, why didn't you ride back with Denis Eady?'

'Why, where *were* you? How did you know? I never saw you!'

Her wonder and his laughter ran together like spring rills in a thaw. Ethan had the sense of having done something arch and ingenious. To prolong the effect he groped for a dazzling phrase, and brought out, in a growl of rapture: 'Come along.'

He slipped an arm through hers, as Eady had done, and fancied it was faintly pressed against her side; but neither of them moved. It was so dark under the spruces that he could barely see the shape of her head beside his shoulder. He longed to stoop his cheek and rub it against her scarf. He would have liked to stand there with her all night in the blackness. She moved forward a step or two and then paused again above the dip of the Corbury road. Its icy slope, scored by innumerable runners, looked like a mirror scratched by travellers at an inn.

'There was a whole lot of them coasting before the moon set,' she said.

'Would you like to come in and coast with them some night?' he asked.

'Oh, *would* you, Ethan? It would be lovely!'

'We'll come to-morrow if there's a moon.'

She lingered, pressing closer to his side. 'Ned Hale and Ruth Varnum came just as *near* running into the big elm at the bottom. We were all sure they were killed.' Her shiver ran down his arm. 'Wouldn't it have been too awful? They're so happy!'

'Oh, Ned ain't much at steering. I guess I can take you down all right!' he said disdainfully.

He was aware that he was 'talking big', like Denis Eady; but his reaction of joy had unsteadied him, and the inflection with which she had said of the engaged couple 'They're so happy!' made the words sound as if she had been thinking of herself and him.

'The elm *is* dangerous, though. It ought to be cut down,' she insisted.

'Would you be afraid of it, with me?'

'I told you I ain't the kind to be afraid,' she tossed back, almost indifferently; and suddenly she began to walk on with a rapid step.

These alterations of mood were the despair and joy of Ethan Frome. The motions of her mind were as incalculable as the flit of a bird in the branches. The fact that he had no right to show his feelings, and thus provoke the expression of hers, made him attach a fantastic importance to every change in her look and tone. Now he thought she understood him, and feared; now he was sure she did not, and despaired. To-night the pressure of accumulated misgivings sent the scale drooping toward despair, and her indifference was the more chilling after the flush of joy into which she had plunged him by dismissing Denis Eady. He mounted School House Hill at her side and walked on in silence till they reached the lane leading to the saw-mill; then the need of some definite assurance grew too strong for him.

'You'd have found me right off if you hadn't gone back to have that last reel with Denis,' he brought out awkwardly. He could not pronounce the name without a stiffening of the muscles of his throat.

'Why, Ethan, how could I tell you were there?'

'I suppose what folks say is true,' he jerked out at her, instead of answering.

She stopped short, and he felt, in the darkness, that her face was lifted quickly to his. 'Why, what do folks say?'

'It's natural enough you should be leaving us,' he floundered on, following his thought.

'Is that what they say?' she mocked back at him; then, with a sudden drop of her sweet treble: 'You mean that Zeena – ain't suited with me any more?' she faltered.

Their arms had slipped apart and they stood motionless, each seeking to distinguish the other's face.

'I know I ain't anything like as smart as I ought to be,' she went on, while he vainly struggled for expression. 'There's lots of things a hired girl could do that come awkward to me still – and I haven't got much strength in my arms. But if she'd only tell me I'd try. You know she hardly ever says anything, and sometimes I can see she ain't suited, and yet I don't know why.' She turned on him with a sudden flash of indignation. 'You'd ought to tell me, Ethan Frome – you'd ought to! Unless *you* want me to go too — '

Unless he wanted her to go too! The cry was balm to his raw wound. The iron heavens seemed to melt and rain down sweetness. Again he struggled for the all-expressive word, and again, his arm in hers, found only a deep 'Come along.'

They walked on in silence through the blackness of the hemlock-shaded lane, where Ethan's saw-mill gloomed through the night, and out again into the comparative clearness of the fields. On the farther side of the hemlock belt* the open country rolled away before them grey and lonely under the stars. Sometimes their way led them under the shade of an overhanging bank or through the thin obscurity of a clump of leafless trees. Here and there a farm-house stood far back among the fields, mute and cold as a grave-stone. The night was so still that they heard the frozen snow crackle under their feet. The crash of a loaded branch falling far off in the woods reverberated like a musket-shot, and once a fox barked, and Mattie shrank closer to Ethan, and quickened her steps.

At length they sighted the group of larches at Ethan's gate, and as they drew near it the sense that the walk was over brought back his words.

'Then you don't want to leave us, Matt?'

He had to stoop his head to catch her stifled whisper: 'Where'd I go, if I did?'

The answer sent a pang through him but the tone suffused him with joy. He forgot what else he had meant to say and pressed her against him so closely that he seemed to feel her warmth in his veins.

'You ain't crying are you, Matt?'

'No, of course I'm not,' she quavered.

They turned in at the gate and passed under the shaded knoll where, enclosed in a low fence, the Frome grave-stones slanted at crazy angles through the snow. Ethan looked at them curiously. For years that quiet company had mocked his restlessness, his desire for change and freedom. 'We never got away – how should you?' seemed to be written on every headstone; and whenever he went in or out of his gate he thought with a shiver: 'I shall just go on living here till I join them.' But now all desire for change had vanished, and the sight of the little enclosure gave him a warm sense of continuance and stability.

'I guess we'll never let you go, Matt,' he whispered, as though even the dead, lovers once, must conspire with him to keep her; and brushing by the graves, he thought: 'We'll always go on living here together, and some day she'll lie there beside me.'

He let the vision possess him as they climbed the hill to the house. He was never so happy with her as when he abandoned himself to these dreams. Half-way up the slope Mattie stumbled against some unseen obstruction and clutched his sleeve to steady herself. The wave of warmth that went through him was like the prolongation of his vision. For the first time he stole his arms about her, and she did not resist. They walked on as if they were floating on a summer stream.

Zeena always went to bed as soon as she had had her supper, and the shutterless windows of the house were dark. A dead cucumber-vine dangled from the porch like the crape streamer tied to the door for a death, and the thought flashed through Ethan's brain: 'If it was there for Zeena—' Then he had a distinct sight of his wife lying in their bedroom asleep, her mouth slightly open, her false teeth in a tumbler by the bed …

They walked around to the back of the house, between the rigid gooseberry bushes. It was Zeena's habit, when they came back late from the village, to leave the key of the kitchen door under the mat. Ethan stood before the door, his head heavy with dreams, his arm still about Mattie. 'Matt—' he began, not knowing what he meant to say.

She slipped out of his hold without speaking, and he stooped down and felt for the key.

'It's not there!' he said, straightening himself with a start.

They strained their eyes at each other through the icy darkness. Such a thing had never happened before.

'Maybe she's forgotten it,' Mattie said in a tremulous whisper; but both of them knew that it was not like Zeena to forget.

'It might have fallen off into the snow,' Mattie continued, after a pause during which they had stood intently listening.

'It must have been pushed off, then,' he rejoined in the same tone. Another wild thought tore through him. What if tramps had been there – what if ...

Again he listened, fancying he heard a distant sound in the house; then he felt in his pocket for a match, and kneeling down, passed its light slowly over the rough edges of snow about the doorstep.

He was still kneeling when his eyes, on a level with the lower panel of the door, caught a faint ray beneath it. Who could be stirring in that silent house? He heard a step on the stairs, and again for an instant the thought of tramps tore through him. Then the door opened and he saw his wife.

Against the dark background of the kitchen she stood up tail and angular, one hand drawing a quilted counterpane° to her flat breast, while the other held a lamp. The light, on a level with her chin, drew out of the darkness her puckered throat and the projecting wrist of the hand that clutched the quilt, and deepened fantastically the hollows and prominences of her high-boned face under its ring of crimping-pins.° To Ethan, still in the rosy haze of his hour with Mattie, the sight came with the intense precision of the last dream before waking. He felt as if he had never before known what his wife looked like.

She drew aside without speaking, and Mattie and Ethan passed into the kitchen, which had the deadly chill of a vault after the dry cold of the night.

'Guess you forgot about us, Zeena,' Ethan joked, stamping the snow from his boots.

'No. I just felt so mean I couldn't sleep.'

Mattie came forward, unwinding her wraps, the colour of the cherry scarf in her fresh lips and cheeks. 'I'm so sorry, Zeena! Isn't there anything I can do?'

'No; there's nothing.' Zeena turned away from her. 'You might 'a' shook off that snow outside,' she said to her husband.

She walked out of the kitchen ahead of them and pausing in the hall raised the lamp at arm's-length, as if to light them up the stairs.

Ethan paused also, affecting to fumble for the peg on which he hung his coat and cap. The doors of the two bedrooms faced each other across the narrow upper landing, and to-night it was peculiarly repugnant to him that Mattie should see him follow Zeena.

'I guess I won't come up yet awhile,' he said, turning as if to go back to the kitchen.

Zeena stopped short and looked at him. 'For the land's sake – what you going to do down here?'

'I've got the mill accounts to go over.'

She continued to stare at him, the flame of the unshaded lamp bringing out with microscopic cruelty the fretful lines of her face.

'At this time o' night? You'll ketch your death. The fire's out long ago.'

Without answering he moved away toward the kitchen. As he did so his glance crossed Mattie's and he fancied that a fugitive warning gleamed through her lashes. The next moment they sank to her flushed cheeks and she began to mount the stairs ahead of Zeena.

'That's so. It *is* powerful cold down here,' Ethan assented; and with lowered head he went up in his wife's wake, and followed her across the threshold of their room.

Chapter 3

There was some hauling to be done at the lower end of the wood-lot, and Ethan was out early the next day.

The winter morning was as clear as crystal. The sunrise burned red in a pure sky, the shadows on the rim of the wood-lot were darkly blue, and beyond the white and scintillating fields patches of far-off forest hung like smoke.

It was in the early morning stillness, when his muscles were swinging to their familiar task and his lungs expanding with long draughts of mountain air, that Ethan did his clearest thinking. He and Zeena had not exchanged a word after the door of their room had closed on them. She had measured out some drops from a medicine-bottle on a chair by the bed and, after swallowing them, and wrapping her head in a piece of yellow flannel, had lain down with her face turned away. Ethan undressed hurriedly and blew out the light so that he should not see her when he took his place at her side. As he lay there he could hear Mattie moving about in her room, and her candle, sending its small ray across the landing, drew a scarcely perceptible line of light under his door. He kept his eyes fixed on the light till it vanished. Then the room grew perfectly black, and not a sound was audible but Zeena's asthmatic breathing. Ethan felt confusedly that there were many things he ought to think about, but through his tingling veins and tired brain only one sensation throbbed: the warmth of Mattie's shoulder against his. Why had he not kissed her when he held her there? A few hours earlier he would not have asked himself the question. Even a few minutes earlier, when they had stood alone outside the house, he would not have dared to think of kissing her. But since he had seen her lips in the lamplight he felt that they were his.

Now, in the bright morning air, her face was still before him. It was part of the sun's red and of the pure glitter on the snow. How the girl had changed since she had come to Starkfield! He remembered what a colourless slip of a thing she had looked the day he had met her at the station. And all the first winter, how she had shivered with cold when the northerly gales shook the thin clapboards and the snow beat like hail against the loose-hung windows!

He had been afraid that she would hate the hard life, the cold and loneliness; but not a sign of discontent escaped her. Zeena took the view that Mattie was bound to make the best of Starkfield since she hadn't any other place to go to; but this did not strike Ethan as conclusive. Zeena, at any rate, did not apply the principle in her own case.

He felt all the more sorry for the girl because misfortune had, in a sense, indentured her to them. Mattie Silver was the daughter of a cousin of Zenobia Frome's, who had inflamed his clan with mingled sentiments of envy and admiration by descending from the hills to Connecticut, where he had married a Stamford girl and succeeded to her father's thriving 'drug' business. Unhappily Orin Silver, a man of far-reaching aims, had died too soon to prove that the end justifies the means. His accounts revealed merely what the means had been; and these were such that it was fortunate for his wife and daughter that his books were examined only after his impressive funeral. His wife died of the disclosure, and Mattie, at twenty, was left alone to make her way on the fifty dollars obtained from the sale of her piano. For this purpose her equipment, though varied, was inadequate. She could trim a hat, make molasses candy, recite 'Curfew shall not ring to-night',⬦ and play 'The Lost Chord'⬦ and a pot-pourri from 'Carmen'.⬦ When she tried to extend the field of her activities in the direction of stenography⬦ and book-keeping her health broke down, and six months on her feet behind the counter of a department store did not tend to restore it. Her nearest relations had been induced to place their savings in her father's hands, and though, after his death, they ungrudgingly acquitted themselves of the Christian duty of returning good for evil by giving his daughter all the advice at their disposal, they could hardly be expected to supplement it by material aid. But when Zenobia's doctor recommended her looking about for some one to help her with the house-work the clan instantly saw the chance of exacting a compensation from Mattie. Zenobia, though doubtful of the girl's efficiency, was tempted by the freedom to find fault without much risk of losing her; and so Mattie came to Starkfield.

Zenobia's fault-finding was of the silent kind, but not the less penetrating for that. During the first months Ethan alternately burned with the desire to see Mattie defy her and trembled with fear of the result. Then the situation grew less strained. The pure air, and the long summer hours in the open, gave back life and elasticity to Mattie, and Zeena, with more leisure to devote to her complex ailments, grew less watchful of the girl's omissions; so that Ethan, struggling on under the burden of his barren farm and failing saw-mill, could at least imagine that peace reigned in his house.

There was really, even now, no tangible evidence to the contrary; but since the previous night a vague dread had hung on his sky-line. It was formed of Zeena's obstinate silence, of Mattie's sudden look of warning, of the memory of just such fleeting imperceptible signs as those which told him, on certain stainless mornings, that before night there would be rain.

His dread was so strong that, man-like, he sought to postpone certainty. The hauling was not over till mid-day, and as the lumber was to be delivered to Andrew Hale, the Starkfield builder, it was really easier for Ethan to send Jotham Powell, the hired man, back to the farm on foot, and drive the load down to the village himself. He had scrambled up on the logs, and was sitting astride of them, close over his shaggy greys, when, coming between him and their streaming necks, he had a vision of the warning look that Mattie had given him the night before.

'If there's going to be any trouble I want to be there,' was his vague reflection, as he threw to Jotham the unexpected order to unhitch the team and lead them back to the barn.

It was a slow trudge home through the heavy fields, and when the two men entered the kitchen Mattie was lifting the coffee from the stove and Zeena was already at the table. Her husband stopped short at sight of her. Instead of her usual calico wrapper and knitted shawl she wore her best dress of brown merino, and above her thin strands of hair, which still preserved the tight undulations of the crimping-pins, rose a hard perpendicular bonnet, as to which Ethan's clearest notion was that he had to pay five dollars for it at the Bettsbridge Emporium. On the floor beside her stood his old valise and a bandbox wrapped in newspapers.

'Why, where are you going, Zeena?' he exclaimed.

'I've got my shooting pains so bad that I'm going over to Bettsbridge to spend the night with Aunt Martha Pierce and see that new doctor,' she answered in a matter-of-fact tone, as if she had said she was going into the store-room to take a look at the preserves, or up to the attic to go over the blankets.

In spite of her sedentary habits such abrupt decisions were not without precedent in Zeena's history. Twice or thrice before she had suddenly packed Ethan's valise and started off to Bettsbridge, or even Springfield, to seek the advice of some new doctor, and her husband had grown to dread these expeditions because of their cost. Zeena always came back laden with expensive remedies, and her last visit to Springfield had been commemorated by her paying twenty dollars for an electric battery of which she had never been able to learn the use. But for the moment his sense of relief was so great as to preclude all other feelings. He had now no doubt that Zeena had spoken the truth in saying, the night before, that she had sat up because she felt 'too mean' to sleep: her abrupt resolve to seek medical advice showed that, as usual, she was wholly absorbed in her health.

As if expecting a protest, she continued plaintively: 'If you're too busy with the hauling I presume you can let Jotham Powell drive me over with the sorrel* in time to ketch the train at the Flats.'

Her husband hardly heard what she was saying. During the winter months there was no stage between Starkfield and Bettsbridge, and the trains which stopped at Corbury Flats were slow and infrequent. A rapid calculation showed Ethan that Zeena could not be back at the farm before the following evening …

'If I'd supposed you'd 'a' made any objection to Jotham Powell's driving me over – ' she began again, as though his silence had implied refusal. On the brink of departure she was always seized with a flux of words. 'All I know is,' she continued, 'I can't go on the way I am much longer. The pains are clear away down to my ankles now, or I'd 'a' walked in to Starkfield on my own feet, sooner'n put you out, and asked Michael Eady to let me ride over on his wagon to the Flats, when he sends to meet the train that brings his groceries. I'd 'a' had two hours to wait in the station, but I'd sooner 'a' done it, even with this cold, than to have you say — '

'Of course Jotham'll drive you over,' Ethan roused himself to answer. He became suddenly conscious that he was looking at Mattie while Zeena talked to him, and with an effort he turned his eyes to his wife. She sat opposite the window, and the pale light reflected from the banks of snow made her face look more than usually drawn and bloodless, sharpened the three parallel creases between ear and cheek, and drew querulous lines from her thin nose to the corners of her mouth. Though she was but seven years her husband's senior, and he was only twenty-eight, she was already an old woman.

Ethan tried to say something befitting the occasion, but there was only one thought in his mind: the fact that, for the first time since Mattie had come to live with them, Zeena was to be away for a night. He wondered if the girl were thinking of it too …

He knew that Zeena must be wondering why he did not offer to drive her to the Flats and let Jotham Powell take the lumber to Starkfield, and at first he could not think of a pretext for not doing so; then he said: 'I'd take you over myself, only I've got to collect the cash for the lumber.'

As soon as the words were spoken he regretted them, not only because they were untrue – there being no prospect of his receiving cash payment from Hale – but also because he knew from experience the imprudence of letting Zeena think he was in funds on the eve of one of her therapeutic excursions. At the moment, however, his one desire was to avoid the long drive with her behind the ancient sorrel who never went out of a walk.

Zeena made no reply: she did not seem to hear what he had said. She had already pushed her plate aside, and was measuring out a draught from a large bottle at her elbow.

'It ain't done me a speck of good, but I guess I might as well use it up,' she remarked; adding, as she pushed the empty bottle toward Mattie: 'If you can get the taste out it'll do for pickles.'

Chapter 4

As soon as his wife had driven off Ethan took his coat and cap from the peg. Mattie was washing up the dishes, humming one of the dance tunes of the night before. He said 'So long, Matt,' and she answered gaily 'So long, Ethan'; and that was all.

It was warm and bright in the kitchen. The sun slanted through the south window on the girl's moving figure, on the cat dozing in a chair, and on the geraniums brought in from the door-way, where Ethan had planted them in the summer to 'make a garden' for Mattie. He would have liked to linger on, watching her tidy up and then settle down to her sewing; but he wanted still more to get the hauling done and be back at the farm before night.

All the way down to the village he continued to think of his return to Mattie. The kitchen was a poor place, not 'spruce' and shining as his mother had kept it in his boyhood; but it was surprising what a homelike look the mere fact of Zeena's absence gave it. And he pictured what it would be like that evening, when he and Mattie were there after supper. For the first time they would be alone together indoors, and they would sit there, one on each side of the stove, like a married couple, he in his stocking feet and smoking his pipe, she laughing and talking in that funny way she had, which was always as new to him as if he had never heard her before.

The sweetness of the picture, and the relief of knowing that his fears of 'trouble' with Zeena were unfounded, sent up his spirits with a rush, and he, who was usually so silent, whistled and sang aloud as he drove through the snowy fields. There was in him a slumbering spark of sociability which the long Starkfield winters had not yet extinguished. By nature grave and inarticulate, he admired recklessness and gaiety in others and was warmed to the marrow by friendly human intercourse. At Worcester, though he had the name of keeping to himself and not being much of a hand at a good time, he had secretly gloried in being clapped on the back and hailed as 'Old Ethe' or 'Old Stiff'; and the cessation of such familiarities had increased the chill of his return to Starkfield.

There the silence had deepened about him year by year. Left alone, after his father's accident, to carry the burden of farm and mill, he had had no time for convivial loiterings in the village; and when his mother fell ill the loneliness of the house grew more oppressive than that of the fields. His mother had been a talker in her day, but after her 'trouble' the sound of her voice was seldom heard, though she had not lost the power of speech. Sometimes, in the long winter evenings, when in desperation her son asked her why she didn't 'say something', she would lift a finger and answer: 'Because I'm listening'; and on stormy nights, when the loud wind was about the house, she would complain, if he spoke to her: 'They're talking so out there that I can't hear you.'

It was only when she drew toward her last illness, and his cousin Zenobia Pierce came over from the next valley to help him nurse her, that human speech was heard again in the house. After the mortal silence of his long imprisonment Zeena's volubility was music in his ears. He felt that he might have 'gone like his mother' if the sound of a new voice had not come to steady him. Zeena seemed to understand his case at a glance. She laughed at him for not knowing the simplest sick-bed duties and told him to 'go right along out' and leave her to see to things. The mere fact of obeying her orders, of feeling free to go about his business again and talk with other men, restored his shaken balance and magnified his sense of what he owed her. Her efficiency shamed and dazzled him. She seemed to possess by instinct all the household wisdom that his long apprenticeship had not instilled in him. When the end came it was she who had to tell him to hitch up and go for the undertaker, and she thought it 'funny' that he had not

60

settled beforehand who was to have his mother's clothes and the sewing-machine. After the funeral, when he saw her preparing to go away, he was seized with an unreasoning dread of being left alone on the farm; and before he knew what he was doing he had asked her to stay there with him. He had often thought since that it would not have happened if his mother had died in spring instead of winter ...

When they married it was agreed that, as soon as he could straighten out the difficulties resulting from Mrs Frome's long illness, they would sell the farm and saw-mill and try their luck in a large town. Ethan's love of nature did not take the form of a taste for agriculture. He had always wanted to be an engineer, and to live in towns, where there were lectures and big libraries and 'fellows doing things'. A slight engineering job in Florida, put in his way during his period of study at Worcester, increased his faith in his ability as well as his eagerness to see the world; and he felt sure that, with a 'smart' wife like Zeena, it would not be long before he had made himself a place in it.

Zeena's native village was slightly larger and nearer to the railway than Starkfield, and she had let her husband see from the first that life on an isolated farm was not what she had expected when she married. But purchasers were slow in coming, and while he waited for them Ethan learned the impossibility of transplanting her. She chose to look down on Starkfield, but she could not have lived in a place which looked down on her. Even Bettsbridge or Shadd's Falls would not have been sufficiently aware of her, and in the greater cities which attracted Ethan she would have suffered a complete loss of identity. And within a year of their marriage she developed the 'sickliness' which had since made her notable even in a community rich in pathological instances. When she came to take care of his mother she had seemed to Ethan like the very genius of health, but he soon saw that her skill as a nurse had been acquired by the absorbed observation of her own symptoms.

Then she too fell silent. Perhaps it was the inevitable effect of life on the farm, or perhaps, as she sometimes said, it was because Ethan 'never listened'. The charge was not wholly unfounded. When she spoke it was only to complain, and to complain of things not in his power to remedy; and to check a tendency to impatient retort he had first formed the habit of not answering her, and finally of thinking of other things while she talked. Of late, however, since he had had reasons for observing her more closely, her silence had begun to trouble him. He recalled his mother's growing taciturnity, and wondered if Zeena were also turning 'queer'. Women did, he knew. Zeena, who had at her fingers' ends the pathological chart of the whole region, had cited many cases of the kind while she was nursing his mother; and he himself knew of certain lonely farm-houses in the neighbourhood where stricken creatures pined, and of others where sudden tragedy had come of their presence. At times, looking at Zeena's shut face, he felt the chill of such forebodings. At other times her silence seemed deliberately assumed to conceal far-reaching intentions, mysterious conclusions drawn from suspicions and resentments impossible to guess. That supposition was even more disturbing than the other; and it was the one which had come to him the night before, when he had seen her standing in the kitchen door.

Now her departure for Bettsbridge had once more eased his mind, and all his thoughts were on the prospect of his evening with Mattie. Only one thing weighed on him, and that was his having told Zeena that he was to receive cash for the lumber. He foresaw so clearly the consequences of this imprudence that with considerable reluctance he decided to ask Andrew Hale for a small advance on his load.

When Ethan drove into Hale's yard the builder was just getting out of his sleigh.

'Hello, Ethe!' he said. 'This comes handy.'

Andrew Hale was a ruddy man with a big grey moustache and a stubbly double-chin unconstrained by a collar; but his scrupulously clean shirt was always fastened by a small diamond stud. This display of opulence was misleading, for though he did a fairly good business it was known that his easygoing habits and the demands of his large family frequently kept him what Starkfield called 'behind'. He was an old friend of Ethan's family, and his house one of the few to which Zeena occasionally went, drawn there by the fact that Mrs Hale, in her youth, had done more 'doctoring' than any other woman in Starkfield, and was still a recognised authority on symptoms and treatment.

Hale went up to the greys and patted their sweating flanks.

'Well, sir,' he said, 'you keep them two as if they was pets.'

Ethan set about unloading the logs and when he had finished his job he pushed open the glazed door of the shed which the builder used as his office. Hale sat with his feet up on the stove, his back propped against a battered desk strewn with papers: the place, like the man, was warm, genial and untidy.

'Sit right down and thaw out,' he greeted Ethan.

The latter did not know how to begin, but at length he managed to bring out his request for an advance of fifty dollars. The blood rushed to his thin skin under the sting of Hale's astonishment. It was the builder's custom to pay at the end of three months, and there was no precedent between the two men for a cash settlement.

Ethan felt that if he had pleaded an urgent need Hale might have made shift to pay him; but pride, and an instinctive prudence, kept him from resorting to this argument. After his father's death it had taken time to get his head above water, and he did not want Andrew Hale, or any one else in Starkfield, to think he was going under again. Besides, he hated lying; if he wanted the money he wanted it, and it was nobody's business to ask why. He therefore made his demand with the awkwardness of a proud man who will not admit to himself that he is stooping; and he was not much surprised at Hale's refusal.

The builder refused genially, as he did everything else: he treated the matter as something in the nature of a practical joke, and wanted to know if Ethan meditated buying a grand piano or adding a 'cupolo' to his house; offering, in the latter case, to give his services free of cost.

Ethan's arts were soon exhausted, and after an embarrassed pause he wished Hale good day and opened the door of the office. As he passed out the builder suddenly called after him: 'See here – you ain't in a tight place, are you?'

'Not a bit,' Ethan's pride retorted before his reason had time to intervene.

'Well, that's good! Because I *am*, a shade. Fact is, I was going to ask you to give me a little extra time on that payment. Business is pretty slack, to begin with, and then I'm fixing up a little house for Ned and Ruth when they're married. I'm glad to do it for 'em, but it costs.' His look appealed to Ethan for sympathy. 'The young people like things nice. You know how it is yourself: it's not so long ago since you fixed up your own place for Zeena.'

Ethan left the greys in Hale's stable and went about some other business in the village. As he walked away the builder's last phrase lingered in his ears, and he reflected grimly that his seven years with Zeena seemed to Starkfield 'not so long'.

The afternoon was drawing to an end, and here and there a lighted pane spangled the cold grey dusk and made the snow look whiter. The bitter weather had driven every one indoors and Ethan had the long rural street to himself. Suddenly he heard the brisk play of sleigh-bells and a cutter passed him, drawn by a free-going horse. Ethan recognised Michael Eady's roan colt, and young Denis Eady, in a handsome new fur cap, leaned forward and waved a greeting. 'Hello, Ethe!' he shouted and spun on.

The cutter was going in the direction of the Frome farm, and Ethan's heart contracted as he listened to the dwindling bells. What more likely than that Denis Eady had heard of Zeena's departure for Bettsbridge, and was profiting by the opportunity to spend an hour with Mattie? Ethan was ashamed of the storm of jealousy in his breast. It seemed unworthy of the girl that his thoughts of her should be so violent.

He walked on to the church corner and entered the shade of the Varnum spruces, where he had stood with her the night before. As he passed into their gloom he saw an indistinct outline just ahead of him. At his approach it melted for an instant into two separate shapes and then conjoined again, and he heard a kiss, and a half-laughing 'Oh!' provoked by the discovery of his presence. Again the outline hastily disunited and the Varnum gate slammed on one half while the other hurried on ahead of him. Ethan smiled at the discomfiture he had caused. What did it matter to Ned Hale and Ruth Varnum if they were caught kissing each other? Everybody in Starkfield knew they were engaged. It pleased Ethan to have surprised a pair of lovers on the spot where he and Mattie had stood with such a thirst for each other in their hearts; but he felt a pang at the thought that these two need not hide their happiness.

He fetched the greys from Hale's stable and started on his long climb back to the farm. The cold was less sharp than earlier in the day and a thick fleecy sky threatened snow for the morrow. Here and there a star pricked through, showing behind it a deep well of blue. In an hour or two the moon would push over the ridge behind the farm, burn a gold-edged rent in the clouds, and then be swallowed by them. A mournful peace hung on the fields, as though they felt the relaxing grasp of the cold and stretched themselves in their long winter sleep.

Ethan's ears were alert for the jingle of sleigh-bells, but not a sound broke the silence of the lonely road. As he drew near the farm he saw, through the thin screen of larches at the gate, a light twinkling in the house above him. 'She's up in her room,' he said to himself, 'fixing herself up for supper;' and he remembered Zeena's sarcastic stare when Mattie, on the evening of her arrival, had come down to supper with smoothed hair and a ribbon at her neck.

He passed by the graves on the knoll and turned his head to glance at one of the older headstones, which had interested him deeply as a boy because it bore his name:

SACRED TO THE MEMORY OF
ETHAN FROME AND ENDURANCE HIS WIFE,
WHO DWELLED TOGETHER IN PEACE
FOR FIFTY YEARS.

He used to think that fifty years sounded like a long time to live together, but now it seemed to him that they might pass in a flash. Then, with a sudden dart of irony, he wondered if, when their turn came, the same epitaph would be written over him and Zeena.

He opened the barn-door and craned his head into the obscurity, half-fearing to discover Denis Eady's roan colt in the stall beside the sorrel. But the old horse was there alone, mumbling his crib with toothless jaws, and Ethan whistled cheerfully while he bedded down the greys and shook an extra measure of oats into their mangers. His was not a tuneful throat, but harsh melodies burst from it as he locked the barn and sprang up the hill to the house. He reached the kitchen-porch and turned the door-handle; but the door did not yield to his touch.

Startled at finding it locked he rattled the handle violently; then he reflected that Mattie was alone and that it was natural she should barricade herself at nightfall. He stood in the darkness expecting to hear her step. It did not come, and after vainly straining his ears he called out in a voice that shook with joy: 'Hello, Matt!'

Silence answered; but in a minute or two he caught a sound on the stairs and saw a line of light about the door-frame, as he had seen it the night before. So strange was the precision with which the incidents of the previous evening were repeating themselves that he half expected, when he heard the key turn, to see his wife before him on the threshold; but the door opened, and Mattie faced him.

She stood just as Zeena had stood, a lifted lamp in her hand, against the black background of the kitchen. She held the light at the same level, and it drew out with the same distinctness her slim young throat and the brown wrist no bigger than a child's. Then, striking upward, it threw a lustrous fleck on her lips, edged her eyes with velvet shade, and laid a milky whiteness above the black curve of her brows.

She wore her usual dress of darkish stuff, and there was no bow at her neck; but through her hair she had run a streak of crimson ribbon. This tribute to the unusual transformed and glorified her. She seemed to Ethan taller, fuller, more womanly in shape and motion. She stood aside, smiling silently, while he entered, and then moved away from him with something soft and flowing in her gait. She set the lamp on the table, and he saw that it was carefully laid for supper, with fresh doughnuts, stewed blueberries and his favourite pickles in a dish of gay red glass. A bright fire glowed in the stove and the cat lay stretched before it, watching the table with a drowsy eye.

Ethan was suffocated with the sense of well-being. He went out into the passage to hang up his coat and pull off his wet boots. When he came back Mattie had set the teapot on the table and the cat was rubbing itself persuasively against her ankles.

'Why, Puss! I nearly tripped over you,' she cried, the laughter sparkling through her lashes.

Again Ethan felt a sudden twinge of jealousy. Could it be his coming that gave her such a kindled face?

'Well, Matt, any visitors?' he threw off, stooping down carelessly to examine the fastening of the stove.

She nodded and laughed 'Yes, one,' and he felt a blackness settling on his brows.

'Who was that?' he questioned, raising himself up to slant a glance at her beneath his scowl.

Her eyes danced with malice. 'Why, Jotham Powell. He came in after he got back, and asked for a drop of coffee before he went down home.'

The blackness lifted and light flooded Ethan's brain. 'That all? Well, I hope you made out to let him have it.' And after a pause he felt it right to add: 'I suppose he got Zeena over to the Flats all right?'

'Oh, yes; in plenty of time.'

The name threw a chill between them, and they stood a moment looking sideways at each other before Mattie said with a shy laugh: 'I guess it's about time for supper.'

They drew their seats up to the table, and the cat, unbidden, jumped between them into Zeena's empty chair. 'Oh, Puss!' said Mattie, and they laughed again.

Ethan, a moment earlier, had felt himself on the brink of eloquence; but the mention of Zeena had paralysed him. Mattie seemed to feel the contagion of his embarrassment, and sat with downcast lids, sipping her tea, while he feigned an insatiable appetite for doughnuts and sweet pickles. At last, after casting about for an effective opening, he took a long gulp of tea, cleared his throat, and said: 'Looks as if there'd be more snow.'

She feigned great interest. 'Is that so? Do you suppose it'll interfere with Zeena's getting back?' She flushed red as the question escaped her, and hastily set down the cup she was lifting.

Ethan reached over for another helping of pickles. 'You never can tell, this time of year, it drifts so bad on the Flats.' The name had benumbed him again, and once more he felt as if Zeena were in the room between them.

'Oh, Puss, you're too greedy!' Mattie cried.

The cat, unnoticed, had crept up on muffled paws from Zeena's seat to the table, and was stealthily elongating its body in the direction of the milk-jug, which stood between Ethan and Mattie. The two leaned forward at the same moment and their hands met on the handle of the jug. Mattie's hand was underneath, and Ethan kept his clasped on it a moment longer than was necessary. The cat, profiting by this unusual demonstration, tried to effect an unnoticed retreat, and in doing so backed into the pickle-dish, which fell to the floor with a crash.

Mattie, in an instant, had sprung from her chair and was down on her knees by the fragments.

'Oh, Ethan, Ethan – it's all to pieces! What will Zeena say?'

But this time his courage was up. 'Well, she'll have to say it to the cat, any way!' he rejoined with a laugh, kneeling down at Mattie's side to scrape up the swimming pickles.

She lifted stricken eyes to him. 'Yes, but, you see, she never meant it should be used, not even when there was company; and I had to get up on the step-ladder to reach it down from the top shelf of the china-closet, where she keeps it with all her best things, and of course she'll want to know why I did it—'

The case was so serious that it called forth all of Ethan's latent resolution.

'She needn't know anything about it if you keep quiet. I'll get another just like it to-morrow. Where did it come from? I'll go to Shadd's Falls for it if I have to!'

'Oh, you'll never get another even there! It was a wedding present – don't you remember? It came all the way from Philadelphia, from Zeena's aunt that married the minister.

That's why she wouldn't ever use it. Oh, Ethan, Ethan, what in the world shall I do?'

She began to cry, and he felt as if every one of her tears were pouring over him like burning lead. 'Don't, Matt, don't – oh, *don't!*' he implored her.

She struggled to her feet, and he rose and followed her helplessly while she spread out the pieces of glass on the kitchen dresser. It seemed to him as if the shattered fragments of their evening lay there.

'Here, give them to me,' he said in a voice of sudden authority.

She drew aside, instinctively obeying his tone. 'Oh, Ethan, what are you going to do?'

Without replying he gathered the pieces of glass into his broad palm and walked out of the kitchen to the passage. There he lit a candle-end, opened the china-closet, and, reaching his long arm up to the highest shelf, laid the pieces together with such accuracy of touch that a close inspection convinced him of the impossibility of detecting from below that the dish was broken. If he glued it together the next morning months might elapse before his wife noticed what had happened, and meanwhile he might after all be able to match the dish at Shadd's Falls or Bettsbridge. Having satisfied himself that there was no risk of immediate discovery he went back to the kitchen with a lighter step, and found Mattie disconsolately removing the last scraps of pickle from the floor.

'It's all right, Matt. Come back and finish supper,' he commanded her.

Completely reassured, she shone on him through tear-hung lashes, and his soul swelled with pride as he saw how his tone subdued her. She did not even ask what he had done. Except when he was steering a big log down the mountain to his mill he had never known such a thrilling sense of mastery.

Chapter 5

They finished supper, and while Mattie cleared the table Ethan went to look at the cows and then took a last turn about the house. The earth lay dark under a muffled sky and the air was so still that now and then he heard a lump of snow come thumping down from a tree far off on the edge of the wood-lot.

When he returned to the kitchen Mattie had pushed up his chair to the stove and seated herself near the lamp with a bit of sewing. The scene was just as he had dreamed of it that morning. He sat down, drew his pipe from his pocket and stretched his feet to the glow. His hard day's work in the keen air made him feel at once lazy and light of mood, and he had a confused sense of being in another world, where all was warmth and harmony and time could bring no change. The only drawback to his complete well-being was the fact that he could not see Mattie from where he sat; but he was too indolent to move and after a moment he said: 'Come over here and sit by the stove.'

Zeena's empty rocking-chair stood facing him. Mattie rose obediently, and seated herself in it. As her young brown head detached itself against the patch-work cushion that habitually framed his wife's gaunt countenance, Ethan had a momentary shock. It was almost as if the other face, the face of the superseded woman, had obliterated that of the intruder. After a moment Mattie seemed to be affected by the same sense of constraint. She changed her position leaning forward to bend her head above her work, so that he saw only the foreshortened tip of her nose and the streak of red in her hair; then she slipped to her feet, saying 'I can't see to sew,' and went back to her chair by the lamp.

Ethan made a pretext of getting up to replenish the stove, and when he returned to his seat he pushed it sideways that he might get a view of her profile and of the lamplight falling on her hands. The cat, who had been a puzzled observer of these unusual movements, jumped up into Zeena's chair, rolled itself into a ball, and lay watching them with narrowed eyes.

Deep quiet sank on the room. The clock ticked above the dresser, a piece of charred wood fell now and then in the stove, and the faint sharp scent of the geraniums mingled with the odour of Ethan's smoke, which began to throw a blue haze about the lamp and to hang its greyish cobwebs in the shadowy corners of the room.

All constraint had vanished between the two, and they began to talk easily and simply. They spoke of every-day things, of the prospect of snow, of the next church sociable, of the loves and quarrels of Starkfield. The commonplace nature of what they said produced in Ethan an illusion of long-established intimacy which no outburst of emotion could have given, and he set his imagination adrift on the fiction that they had always spent their evenings thus and would always go on doing so ...

'This is the night we were to have gone coasting, Matt,' he said at length, with the rich sense, as he spoke, that they could go on any other night they chose, since they had all time before them.

She smiled back at him. 'I guess you forgot!'

'No, I didn't forget; but it's as dark as Egypt outdoors. We might go to-morrow if there's a moon.'

She laughed with pleasure, her head tilted back, the lamplight sparkling on her lips and teeth. 'That would be lovely, Ethan!'

He kept his eyes fixed on her, marvelling at the way her face changed with each turn of their talk, like a wheat-field under a summer breeze. It was intoxicating to find such magic in his clumsy words, and he longed to try new ways of using it.

'Would you be scared to go down the Corbury road with me on a night like this?' he asked.

Her cheeks burned redder. 'I ain't any more scared than you are!'

'Well, *I'd* be scared, then; I wouldn't do it. That's an ugly corner down by the big elm. If a fellow didn't keep his eyes open he'd go plumb into it.' He luxuriated in the sense of protection and authority which his words conveyed. To prolong and intensify the feeling he added: 'I guess we're well enough here.'

She let her lids sink slowly, in the way he loved. 'Yes, we're well enough here,' she sighed.

Her tone was so sweet that he took the pipe from his mouth and drew his chair up to the table. Leaning forward, he touched the farther end of the strip of brown stuff that she was hemming. 'Say, Matt,' he began with a smile, 'what do you think I saw under the Varnum spruces, coming along home just now? I saw a friend of yours getting kissed.'

The words had been on his tongue all the evening, but now that he had spoken them they struck him as inexpressibly vulgar and out of place.

Mattie blushed to the roots of her hair and pulled her needle rapidly twice or thrice through her work, insensibly drawing the end of it away from him. 'I suppose it was Ruth and Ned,' she said in a low voice, as though he had suddenly touched on something grave.

Ethan had imagined that his allusion might open the way to the accepted pleasantries, and these perhaps in turn to a harmless caress, if only a mere touch on her hand. But now he felt as if her blush had set a flaming guard about her. He supposed it was his natural awkwardness that made him feel so. He knew that most young men made nothing at all of giving a pretty girl a kiss, and he remembered that the night before, when he had put his arm about Mattie, she had not resisted. But that had been out-of-doors, under the open irresponsible night. Now, in the warm lamplit room, with all its ancient implications of conformity and order, she seemed infinitely farther away from him and more unapproachable.

To ease his constraint he said: 'I suppose they'll be setting a date before long.'

'Yes. I shouldn't wonder if they got married some time along in the summer.' She pronounced the word *married* as if her voice caressed it. It seemed a rustling covert leading to enchanted glades. A pang shot through Ethan, and he said, twisting away from her in his chair: 'It'll be your turn next, I wouldn't wonder.'

She laughed a little uncertainly. 'Why do you keep on saying that?'

He echoed her laugh. 'I guess I do it to get used to the idea.'

He drew up to the table again and she sewed on in silence, with dropped lashes, while he sat in fascinated contemplation of the way in which her hands went up and down above the strip of stuff, just as he had seen a pair of birds make short perpendicular flights over a nest they were building. At length, without turning her head or lifting her lids, she said in a low tone: 'It's not because you think Zeena's got anything against me, is it?'

His former dread started up full-armed at the suggestion. 'Why, what do you mean?' he stammered.

She raised distressed eyes to his, her work dropping on the table between them. 'I don't know. I thought last night she seemed to have.'

'I'd like to know what,' he growled.

'Nobody can tell with Zeena.' It was the first time they had ever spoken so openly of her attitude toward Mattie, and the repetition of the name seemed to carry it to the farther corners of the room and send it back to them in long repercussions of sound. Mattie waited, as if to give the echo time to drop, and then went on: 'She hasn't said anything to *you*?'

He shook his head. 'No, not a word.'

She tossed the hair back from her forehead with a laugh. 'I guess I'm just nervous, then. I'm not going to think about it any more.'

'Oh, no – don't let's think about it, Matt!'

The sudden heat of his tone made her colour mount again, not with a rush, but gradually, delicately, like the reflection of a thought stealing slowly across her heart. She sat silent, her hands clasped on her work, and it seemed to him that a warm current flowed toward him along the strip of stuff that still lay unrolled between them. Cautiously he slid his hand palm-downward along the table till his finger-tips touched the end of the stuff. A faint vibration of her lashes seemed to show that she was aware of his gesture, and that it had sent a counter-current back to her; and she let her hands lie motionless on the other end of the strip.

As they sat thus he heard a sound behind him and turned his head. The cat had jumped from Zeena's chair to dart at a mouse in the wainscot, and as a result of the sudden movement the empty chair had set up a spectral rocking.

'She'll be rocking in it herself this time to-morrow,' Ethan thought. 'I've been in a dream, and this is the only evening we'll ever have together.' The return to reality was as painful as the return to consciousness after taking an anæsthetic. His body and brain ached with indescribable weariness, and he could think of nothing to say or to do that should arrest the mad flight of the moments.

His alteration of mood seemed to have communicated itself to Mattie. She looked up at him languidly, as though her lids were weighted with sleep and it cost her an effort to raise them. Her glance fell on his hand, which now completely covered the end of her work and grasped it as if it were a part of herself. He saw a scarcely perceptible tremor cross her face, and without knowing what he did he stooped his head and kissed the bit of stuff in his hold. As his lips rested on it he felt it glide slowly from beneath them, and saw that Mattie had risen and was silently rolling up her work. She fastened it with a pin, and then, finding her thimble and scissors, put them with the roll of stuff into the box covered with fancy paper which he had once brought to her from Bettsbridge.

He stood up also, looking vaguely about the room. The clock above the dresser struck eleven.

'Is the fire all right?' she asked in a low voice.

He opened the door of the stove and poked aimlessly at the embers. When he raised himself again he saw that she was dragging toward the stove the old soap-box lined with carpet in which the cat made its bed. Then she recrossed the floor and lifted two of the geranium pots in her arms, moving them away from the cold window. He followed her and brought the other geraniums, the hyacinth bulbs in a cracked custard bowl and the German ivy trained over an old croquet hoop.

When these nightly duties were performed there was nothing left to do but to bring in the tin candlestick from the passage, light the candle and blow out the lamp. Ethan put the candlestick in Mattie's hand and she went out of the kitchen ahead of him, the light that she carried before her making her dark hair look like a drift of mist on the moon.

'Good night, Matt,' he said as she put her foot on the first step of the stairs.

She turned and looked at him a moment. 'Good night, Ethan,' she answered, and went up.

When the door of her room had closed on her he remembered that he had not even touched her hand.

Chapter 6

The next morning at breakfast Jotham Powell was between them, and Ethan tried to hide his joy under an air of exaggerated indifference, lounging back in his chair to throw scraps to the cat, growling at the weather, and not so much as offering to help Mattie when she rose to clear away the dishes.

He did not know why he was so irrationally happy, for nothing was changed in his life or hers. He had not even touched the tip of her fingers or looked her full in the eyes. But their evening together had given him a vision of what life at her side might be, and he was glad now that he had done nothing to trouble the sweetness of the picture. He had a fancy that she knew what had restrained him ...

There was a last load of lumber to be hauled to the village, and Jotham Powell—who did not work regularly for Ethan in winter—had 'come round' to help with the job. But a wet snow, melting to sleet, had fallen in the night and turned the roads to glass. There was more wet in the air and it seemed likely to both men that the weather would 'milden' toward afternoon and make the going safer. Ethan therefore proposed to his assistant that they should load the sledge at the wood-lot, as they had done on the previous morning, and put off the 'teaming' to Starkfield till later in the day. This plan had the advantage of enabling him to send Jotham to the Flats after dinner to meet Zenobia, while he himself took the lumber down to the village.

He told Jotham to go out and harness up the greys, and for a moment he and Mattie had the kitchen to themselves. She had plunged the breakfast dishes into a tin dish-pan and was bending above it with her slim arms bared to the elbow, the steam from the hot water beading her forehead and tightening her rough hair into little brown rings like the tendrils on the traveller's joy.◇

Ethan stood looking at her, his heart in his throat. He wanted to say: 'We shall never be alone again like this.' Instead, he reached down his tobacco-pouch from a shelf of the dresser, put it into his pocket and said: 'I guess I can make out to be home for dinner.'

She answered 'All right, Ethan,' and he heard her singing over the dishes as he went.

As soon as the sledge was loaded he meant to send Jotham back to the farm and hurry on foot into the village to buy the glue for the pickle-dish. With ordinary luck he should have had time to carry out this plan; but everything went wrong from the start. On the way over to the wood-lot one of the greys slipped on a glare of ice and cut his knee; and when they got him up again Jotham had to go back to the barn for a strip of rag to bind the cut. Then, when the loading finally began, a sleety rain was coming down once more, and the tree trunks were so slippery that it took twice as long as usual to lift them and get them in place on the sledge. It was what Jotham called a sour morning for work, and the horses, shivering and stamping under their wet blankets, seemed to like it as little as the men. It was long past the dinner-hour when the job was done, and Ethan had to give up going to the village because he wanted to lead the injured horse home and wash the cut himself.

He thought that by starting out again with the lumber as soon as he had finished his dinner he might get back to the farm with the glue before Jotham and the old sorrel had had time to fetch Zenobia from the Flats; but he knew the chance was a slight one. It turned on the state of the roads and on the possible lateness of the Bettsbridge train. He remembered afterward, with a grim flash of self-derision, what importance he had attached to the weighing of these probabilities ...

As soon as dinner was over he set out again for the wood-lot, not daring to linger till Jotham Powell left. The hired man was still drying his wet feet at the stove, and Ethan could only give Mattie a quick look as he said beneath his breath: 'I'll be back early.'

He fancied that she nodded her comprehension; and with that scant solace he had to trudge off through the rain.

He had driven his load half-way to the village when Jotham Powell overtook him, urging the reluctant sorrel toward the Flats. 'I'll have to hurry up to do it,' Ethan mused, as the sleigh dropped down ahead of him over the dip of the school-house hill. He worked like ten at the unloading, and when it was over hastened on to Michael Eady's for the glue. Eady and his assistant were both 'down street', and young Denis, who seldom deigned to take their place, was lounging by the stove with a knot of the golden youth of Starkfield. They hailed Ethan with ironic compliment and offers of conviviality; but no one knew where to find the glue. Ethan, consumed with the longing for a last moment alone with Mattie, hung about impatiently while Denis made an ineffectual search in the obscurer corners of the store.

'Looks as if we were all sold out. But if you'll wait around till the old man comes along maybe he can put his hand on it.'

'I'm obliged to you, but I'll try if I can get it down at Mrs Homan's,' Ethan answered, burning to be gone.

Denis's commercial instinct compelled him to aver on oath that what Eady's store could not produce would never be found at the widow Homan's; but Ethan, heedless of this boast, had already climbed to the sledge and was driving on to the rival establishment. Here, after considerable search, and sympathetic questions as to what he wanted it for, and whether ordinary flour paste wouldn't do as well if she couldn't find it, the widow Homan finally hunted down her solitary bottle of glue to its hiding-place in a medley of cough-lozenges and corset-laces.

'I hope Zeena ain't broken anything she sets store by,' she called after him as he turned the greys toward home.

The fitful bursts of sleet had changed into a steady rain and the horses had heavy work even without a load behind them. Once or twice, hearing sleigh-bells, Ethan turned his head, fancying that Zeena and Jotham might overtake him; but the old sorrel was not in sight, and he set his face against the rain and urged on his ponderous pair.

The barn was empty when the horses turned into it and, after giving them the most perfunctory ministrations they had ever received from him, he strode up to the house and pushed open the kitchen door.

Mattie was there alone, as he had pictured her. She was bending over a pan on the stove; but at the sound of his step she turned with a start and sprang to him.

'See, here, Matt, I've got some stuff to mend the dish with! Let me get at it quick,' he cried, waving the bottle in one hand while he put her lightly aside; but she did not seem to hear him.

'Oh, Ethan – Zeena's come,' she said in a whisper, clutching his sleeve.

They stood and stared at each other, pale as culprits.

'But the sorrel's not in the barn!' Ethan stammered.

'Jotham Powell brought some goods over from the Flats for his wife, and he drove right on home with them,' she explained.

He gazed blankly about the kitchen, which looked cold and squalid in the rainy winter twilight.

'How is she?' he asked, dropping his voice to Mattie's whisper.

She looked away from him uncertainly. 'I don't know. She went right up to her room.'

'She didn't say anything?'

'No.'

Ethan let out his doubts in a low whistle and thrust the bottle back into his pocket. 'Don't fret; I'll come down and mend it in the night,' he said. He pulled on his wet coat again and went back to the barn to feed the greys.

While he was there Jotham Powell drove up with the sleigh, and when the horses had been attended to Ethan said to him: 'You might as well come back up for a bite.' He was not sorry to assure himself of Jotham's neutralising presence at the supper table, for Zeena was always 'nervous' after a journey. But the hired man, though seldom loth to accept a meal not included in his wages, opened his stiff jaws to answer slowly: 'I'm obliged to you, but I guess I'll go along back.'

Ethan looked at him in surprise. 'Better come up and dry off. Looks as if there'd be something hot for supper.'

Jotham's facial muscles were unmoved by this appeal and, his vocabulary being limited, he merely repeated: 'I guess I'll go along back.'

To Ethan there was something vaguely ominous in this stolid rejection of free food and warmth, and he wondered what had happened on the drive to nerve Jotham to such stoicism. Perhaps Zeena had failed to see the new doctor or had not liked his counsels: Ethan knew that in such cases the first person she met was likely to be held responsible for her grievance.

When he re-entered the kitchen the lamp lit up the same scene of shining comfort as on the previous evening. The table had been as carefully laid, a clear fire glowed in the stove, the cat dozed in its warmth, and Mattie came forward carrying a plate of doughnuts.

She and Ethan looked at each other in silence; then she said, as she had said the night before: 'I guess it's about time for supper.'

Chapter 7

Ethan went out into the passage to hang up his wet garments. He listened for Zeena's step and, not hearing it, called her name up the stairs. She did not answer, and after a moment's hesitation he went up and opened her door. The room was almost dark, but in the obscurity he saw her sitting by the window, bolt upright, and knew by the rigidity of the outline projected against the pane that she had not taken off her travelling dress.

'Well, Zeena,' he ventured from the threshold.

She did not move, and he continued: 'Supper's about ready. Ain't you coming?'

She replied: 'I don't feel as if I could touch a morsel.'

It was the consecrated formula, and he expected it to be followed, as usual, by her rising and going down to supper. But she remained seated, and he could think of nothing more felicitous than: 'I presume you're tired after the long ride.'

Turning her head at this, she answered solemnly: 'I'm a great deal sicker than you think.'

Her words fell on his ear with a strange shock of wonder. He had often heard her pronounce them before – what if at last they were true?

He advanced a step or two into the dim room. 'I hope that's not so, Zeena,' he said.

She continued to gaze at him through the twilight with a mien of wan authority, as of one consciously singled out for a great fate. 'I've got complications,' she said.

Ethan knew the word for one of exceptional import. Almost everybody in the neighbourhood had 'troubles', frankly localized and specified; but only the chosen had 'complications'. To have them in itself a distinction, though it was also, in most cases, a death-warrant. People struggled on for years with 'troubles', but they almost always succumbed to 'complications'.

Ethan's heart was jerking to and fro between two extremities of feeling, but for the moment compassion prevailed. His wife looked so hard and lonely, sitting there in the darkness with such thoughts.

'Is that what the new doctor told you?' he asked, instinctively lowering his voice.

'Yes. He says any regular doctor would want me to have an operation.'

Ethan was aware that, in regard to the important question of surgical intervention, the female opinion of the neighbourhood was divided, some glorying in the prestige conferred by operations while others shunned them as indelicate. Ethan, from motives of economy, had always been glad that Zeena was of the latter faction.

In the agitation caused by the gravity of her announcement he sought a consolatory short cut.

'What do you know about this doctor anyway? Nobody ever told you that before.'

He saw his blunder before she could take it up: she wanted sympathy, not consolation.

'I didn't need to have anybody tell me I was losing ground every day. Everybody but you could see it. And everybody in Bettsbridge knows about Dr Buck. He has his office in Worcester, and comes over once a fortnight to Shadd's Falls and Bettsbridge for consultations. Eliza Spears was wasting away with kidney trouble before she went to him, and now she's up and around, and singing in the choir.'

'Well, I'm glad of that. You must do just what he tells you,' Ethan answered sympathetically.

She was still looking at him. 'I mean to,' she said. He was struck by a new note in her voice. It was neither whining nor reproachful, but drily resolute.

'What does he want you should do?' he asked, with a mounting vision of fresh expenses.

'He wants I should have a hired girl. He says I oughtn't to have to do a single thing around the house.'

'A hired girl?' Ethan stood transfixed.

'Yes. And Aunt Martha found me one right off. Everybody said I was lucky to get a girl to come away out here, and I agreed to give her a dollar extry to make sure. She'll be over to-morrow afternoon.'

Wrath and dismay contended in Ethan. He had foreseen an immediate demand for money, but not a permanent drain on his scant resources. He no longer believed what Zeena had told him of the supposed seriousness of her state: he saw in her expedition to Bettsbridge only a plot hatched between herself and her Pierce relations to foist on him the cost of a servant; and for the moment wrath predominated.

'If you meant to engage a girl you ought to have told me before you started,' he said.

'How could I tell you before I started? How did I know what Dr Buck would say?'

'Oh, Dr Buck — ' Ethan's incredulity escaped in a short laugh. 'Did Dr Buck tell you how I was to pay her wages?'

Her voice rose furiously with his. 'No, he didn't. For I'd 'a' been ashamed to tell *him* that you grudged me the money to get back my health, when I lost it nursing your own mother!'

'*You* lost your health nursing mother?'

'Yes; and my folks all told me at the time you couldn't do no less than marry me after — '

'Zeena!'

Through the obscurity which hid their faces their thoughts seemed to dart at each other like serpents shooting venom. Ethan was seized with horror of the scene and shame at his own share in it. It was as senseless and savage as a physical fight between two enemies in the darkness.

He turned to the shelf above the chimney, groped for matches and lit the one candle in the room. At first its weak flame made no impression on the shadows; then Zeena's face stood grimly out against the uncurtained pane, which had turned from grey to black.

It was the first scene of open anger between the couple in their sad seven years together, and Ethan felt as if he had lost an irretrievable advantage in descending to the level of recrimination. But the practical problem was there and had to be dealt with.

'You know I haven't got the money to pay for a girl, Zeena. You'll have to send her back: I can't do it.'

'The doctor says it'll be my death if I go on slaving the way I've had to. He doesn't understand how I've stood it as long as I have.'

'Slaving! — ' He checked himself again, 'You sha'n't lift a hand, if he says so. I'll do everything round the house myself — '

She broke in: 'You're neglecting the farm enough already,' and this being true, he found no answer, and left her time to add ironically: 'Better send me over to the almshouse and done with it ... I guess there's been Fromes there afore now.'

The taunt burned into him, but he let it pass. 'I haven't got the money. That settles it.'

There was a moment's pause in the struggle, as though the combatants were testing their weapons. Then Zeena said in a level voice: 'I thought you were to get fifty dollars from Andrew Hale for that lumber.'

'Andrew Hale never pays under three months.' He had hardly spoken when he remembered the excuse he had made for not accompanying his wife to the station the day before; and the blood rose to his frowning brows.

'Why, you told me yesterday you'd fixed it up with him to pay cash down. You said that was why you couldn't drive me over to the Flats.'

Ethan had no suppleness in deceiving. He had never before been convicted of a lie, and all the resources of evasion failed him. 'I guess that was a misunderstanding,' he stammered.

'You ain't got the money?'

'No.'

'And you ain't going to get it?'

'No.'

'Well, I couldn't know that when I engaged the girl, could I?'

'No.' He paused to control his voice. 'But you know it now. I'm sorry, but it can't be helped. You're a poor man's wife, Zeena; but I'll do the best I can for you.'

For a while she sat motionless, as if reflecting, her arms stretched along the arms of her chair, her eyes fixed on vacancy. 'Oh, I guess we'll make out,' she said mildly.

The change in her tone reassured him. 'Of course we will! There's a whole lot more I can do for you, and Mattie — '

Zeena, while he spoke, seemed to be following out some elaborate mental calculation. She emerged from it to say: 'There'll be Mattie's board less, anyhow — '

Ethan, supposing the discussion to be over, had turned to go down to supper. He stopped short, not grasping what he heard. 'Mattie's board less — ?' he began.

Zeena laughed. It was an odd unfamiliar sound – he did not remember ever having heard her laugh before. 'You didn't suppose I was going to keep two girls, did you? No wonder you were scared at the expense!'

He still had but a confused sense of what she was saying. From the beginning of the discussion he had instinctively avoided the mention of Mattie's name, fearing he hardly knew what: criticism, complaints, or vague allusions to the imminent probability of her marrying. But the thought of a definite rupture had never come to him, and even now could not lodge itself in his mind.

'I don't know what you mean,' he said. 'Mattie Silver's not a hired girl. She's your relation.'

'She's a pauper that's hung onto us all after her father'd done his best to ruin us. I've kep' her here a whole year: it's somebody else's turn now.'

As the shrill words shot out Ethan heard a tap on the door, which he had drawn shut when he turned back from the threshold.

'Ethan – Zeena!' Mattie's voice sounded gaily from the landing, 'do you know what time it is? Supper's been ready half an hour.'

Inside the room there was a moment's silence; then Zeena called out from her seat: 'I'm not coming down to supper.'

'Oh, I'm sorry! Aren't you well? Sha'n't I bring you up a bite of something?'

Ethan roused himself with an effort and opened the door. 'Go along down, Matt. Zeena's just a little tired. I'm coming.'

He heard her 'All right!' and her quick step on the stairs; then he shut the door and turned back into the room. His wife's attitude was unchanged, her face inexorable, and he was seized with the despairing sense of his helplessness.

'You ain't going to do it, Zeena?'

'Do what?' she emitted between flattened lips.

'Send Mattie away – like this?'

'I never bargained to take her for life!'

He continued with rising vehemence: 'You can't put her out of the house like a thief – a poor girl without friends or money. She's done her best for you and she's got no place to go to. You may forget she's your kin but everybody else'll remember it. If you do a thing like that what do you suppose folks'll say of you?'

Zeena waited a moment, as if giving him time to feel the full force of the contrast between his own excitement and her composure. Then she replied in the same smooth voice: 'I know well enough what they say of my having kep' her here as long as I have.'

Ethan's hand dropped from the door-knob, which he had held clenched since he had drawn the door shut on Mattie. His wife's retort was like a knife-cut across the sinews and he felt suddenly weak and powerless. He had meant to humble himself, to argue that Mattie's keep didn't cost much, after all, that he could make out to buy a stove and fix up a place in the attic for the hired girl – but Zeena's words revealed the peril of such pleadings.

'You mean to tell her she's got to go – at once?' he faltered out, in terror of letting his wife complete her sentence.

As if trying to make him see reason she replied impartially: 'The girl will be over from Bettsbridge to-morrow, and I presume she's got to have somewheres to sleep.'

Ethan looked at her with loathing. She was no longer the listless creature who had lived at his side in a state of sullen self-absorption, but a mysterious alien presence, an evil energy secreted from the long years of silent brooding. It was the sense of his helplessness that sharpened his antipathy. There had never been anything in her that one could appeal to; but as long as he could ignore and command he had remained indifferent. Now she had mastered him and he abhorred her. Mattie was her relation, not his: there were no means by which he could compel her to keep the girl under her roof. All the long misery of his baffled past, of his youth of failure, hardship and vain effort, rose up in his soul in bitterness and seemed to take shape before him in the woman who at every turn had barred his way. She had taken everything else from him; and now she meant to take the one thing that made up for all the others. For a moment such a flame of hate rose in him that it ran down his arm and clenched his fist against her. He took a wild step forward and then stopped.

'You're – you're not coming down?' he said in a bewildered voice.

'No. I guess I'll lay down on the bed a little while,' she answered mildly; and he turned and walked out of the room.

In the kitchen Mattie was sitting by the stove, the cat curled up on her knees. She sprang to her feet as Ethan entered and carried the covered dish of meat-pie to the table.

'I hope Zeena isn't sick?' she asked.

'No.'

She shone at him across the table. 'Well, sit right down then. You must be starving.' She uncovered the pie and pushed it over to him. So they were to have one more evening together, her happy eyes seemed to say!

He helped himself mechanically and began to eat; then disgust took him by the throat and he laid down his fork.

Mattie's tender gaze was on him and she marked the gesture.

'Why, Ethan, what's the matter? Don't it taste right?'

'Yes – it's first-rate. Only I — ' He pushed his plate away, rose from his chair, and walked around the table to her side. She started up with frightened eyes.

'Ethan, there's something wrong! I *knew* there was!'

She seemed to melt against him in her terror, and he caught her in his arms, held her fast there, felt her lashes beat his cheek like netted butterflies.

'What is it – what is it?' she stammered; but he had found her lips at last and was drinking unconsciousness of everything but the joy they gave him.

She lingered a moment, caught in the same strong current; then she slipped from him and drew back a step or two, pale and troubled. Her look smote him with compunction, and he cried out, as if he saw her drowning in a dream: 'You can't go, Matt! I'll never let you!'

'Go – go?' she stammered. 'Must I go?'

The words went on sounding between them as though a torch of warning flew from hand to hand through a black landscape.

Ethan was overcome with shame at his lack of self-control in flinging the news at her so brutally. His head reeled and he had to support himself against the table. All the while he felt as if he were still kissing her, and yet dying of thirst for her lips.

'Ethan, what has happened? Is Zeena mad with me?'

Her cry steadied him, though it deepened his wrath and pity. 'No, no,' he assured her, 'it's not that. But this new doctor has scared her about herself. You know she believes all they say the first time she sees them. And this one's told her she won't get well unless she lays up and don't do a thing about the house – not for months — '

He paused, his eyes wandering from her miserably. She stood silent a moment, drooping before him like a broken branch. She was so small and weak-looking that it wrung his heart; but suddenly she lifted her head and looked straight at him. 'And she wants somebody handier in my place? Is that it?'

'That's what she says to-night.'

'If she says it to-night she'll say it to-morrow.'

Both bowed to the inexorable truth: they knew that Zeena never changed her mind, and that in her case a resolve once taken was equivalent to an act performed.

There was a long silence between them; then Mattie said in a low voice: 'Don't be too sorry, Ethan.'

'Oh, God – oh, God,' he groaned. The glow of passion he had felt for her had melted to an aching tenderness. He saw her quick lids beating back the tears, and longed to take her in his arms and soothe her.

'You're letting your supper get cold,' she admonished him with a pale gleam of gaiety.

'Oh, Matt – Matt – where'll you go to?'

Her lids sank and a tremor crossed her face. He saw that for the first time the thought of the future came to her distinctly. 'I might get something to do over at Stamford,' she faltered, as if knowing that he knew she had no hope.

He dropped beck into his seat and hid his face in his hands. Despair seized him at the thought of her setting out alone to renew the weary quest for work. In the only place where she was known she was surrounded by indifference or animosity; and what chance had she, inexperienced and untrained, among the million bread-seekers of the cities? There came back to him miserable tales he had heard at Worcester, and the faces of girls whose lives had begun as hopefully as Mattie's ... It was not possible to think of such things without a revolt of his whole being. He sprang up suddenly.

'You can't go, Matt! I won't let you! She's always had her way, but I mean to have mine now — '

Mattie lifted her hand with a quick gesture, and he heard his wife's step behind him.

Zeena came into the room with her dragging down-at-the-heel step, and quietly took her accustomed seat between them.

'I felt a little mite better, and Dr Buck says I ought to eat all I can to keep my strength up, even if I ain't got any appetite,' she said in her flat whine, reaching across Mattie for the teapot. Her 'good' dress had been replaced by the black calico and brown knitted shawl which formed her daily wear, and with them she had put on her usual face and manner. She poured out her tea, added a great deal of milk to it, helped herself largely to pie and pickles, and made the familiar gesture of adjusting her false teeth before she began to eat. The cat rubbed itself ingratiatingly against her, and she said 'Good Pussy,' stooped to stroke it and gave it a scrap of meat from her plate.

Ethan sat speechless, not pretending to eat, but Mattie nibbled valiantly at her food and asked Zeena one or two questions about her visit to Bettsbridge. Zeena answered in her every-day tone and, warming to the theme, regaled them with several vivid descriptions of intestinal disturbances among her friends and relatives. She looked straight at Mattie as she spoke, a faint smile deepening the vertical lines between her nose and chin.

When supper was over she rose from her seat and pressed her hand to the flat surface over the region of her heart. 'That pie of yours always sets a mite heavy, Matt,' she said, not ill-naturedly. She seldom abbreviated the girl's name, and when she did so it was always a sign of affability.

'I've a good mind to go and hunt up those stomach powders I got last year over in Springfield,' she continued. 'I ain't tried them for quite a while, and maybe they'll help the heartburn.'

Mattie lifted her eyes. 'Can't I get them for you, Zeena?' she ventured.

'No. They're in a place you don't know about,' Zeena answered darkly, with one of her secret looks.

She went out of the kitchen and Mattie, rising, began to clear the dishes from the table. As she passed Ethan's chair their eyes met and clung together desolately. The warm still kitchen looked as peaceful as the night before. The cat had sprung to Zeena's rocking-chair, and the heat of the fire was beginning to draw out the faint sharp scent of the geraniums. Ethan dragged himself wearily to his feet.

'I'll go out and take a look around,' he said, going toward the passage to get his lantern.

As he reached the door he met Zeena coming back into the room, her lips twitching with anger, a flush of excitement on her sallow face. The shawl had slipped from her shoulders and was dragging at her down-trodden heels, and in her hands she carried the fragments of the red glass pickle-dish.

'I'd like to know who done this,' she said, looking sternly from Ethan to Mattie.

There was no answer, and she continued in a trembling voice: 'I went to get those powders I'd put away in father's old spectacle-case, top of the china-closet, where I keep the things I set store by, so's folks sha'n't meddle with them — ' Her voice broke, and two small tears hung on her lashless lids and ran slowly down her cheeks. 'It takes the step-ladder to get at the top shelf, and I put Aunt Philura Maple's pickle-dish up there o' purpose when we was married, and it's never been down since, 'cept for the spring cleaning, and then I always lifted it with my own hands, so's 't shouldn't get broke.' She laid the fragments reverently on the table. 'I want to know who done this,' she quavered.

At the challenge Ethan turned back into the room and faced her. 'I can tell you, then. The cat done it.'

'The *cat?*'

'That's what I said.'

She looked at him hard, and then turned her eyes to Mattie, who was carrying the dish-pan to the table.

'I'd like to know how the cat got into my china-closet,' she said.

'Chasin' mice, I guess,' Ethan rejoined. 'There was a mouse round the kitchen all last evening.'

Zeena continued to look from one to the other; then she emitted her small strange laugh. 'I knew the cat was a smart cat,' she said in a high voice, 'but I didn't know he was smart enough to pick up the pieces of my pickle-dish and lay 'em edge to edge on the very shelf he knocked 'em off of.'

Mattie suddenly drew her arms out of the steaming water. 'It wasn't Ethan's fault, Zeena! The cat *did* break the dish; but I got it down from the china-closet, and I'm the one to blame for its getting broken.'

Zeena stood beside the ruin of her treasure, stiffening into a stony image of resentment. '*You* got down my pickle-dish – what for?'

A bright flush flew to Mattie's cheeks. 'I wanted to make the supper-table pretty,' she said.

'You wanted to make the supper-table pretty; and you waited till my back was turned, and took the thing I set most store by of anything I've got, and wouldn't never use it, not even when the minister come to dinner, or Aunt Martha Pierce come over from Bettsbridge — ' Zeena paused with a gasp, as if terrified by her own evocation of the sacrilege. 'You're a bad girl, Mattie Silver, and I always known it. It's the way your father begun, and I was warned of it when I took you, and I tried to keep my things where you couldn't get at 'em – and now you've took from me the one I cared for most of all — ' She broke off in a short spasm of sobs that passed and left her more than ever like a shape of stone.

'If I'd 'a' listened to folks, you'd 'a' gone before now, and this wouldn't 'a' happened,' she said; and gathering up the bits of broken glass she went out of the room as if she carried a dead body …

Chapter 8

When Ethan was called back to the farm by his father's illness his mother gave him, for his own use, a small room behind the untenanted 'best parlour'. Here he had nailed up shelves for his books, built himself a box-sofa out of boards and a mattress, laid out his papers on a kitchen-table, hung on the rough plaster wall an engraving of Abraham Lincoln and a calendar with 'Thoughts from the Poets', and tried, with these meagre properties, to produce some likeness to the study of a 'minister' who had been kind to him and lent him books when he was at Worcester. He still took refuge there in summer, but when Mattie came to live at the farm he had had to give her his stove, and consequently the room was uninhabitable for several months of the year.

To this retreat he descended as soon as the house was quiet, and Zeena's steady breathing from the bed had assured him that there was to be no sequel to the scene in the kitchen. After Zeena's departure he and Mattie had stood speechless, neither seeking to approach the other. Then the girl had returned to her task of clearing up the kitchen for the night and he had taken his lantern and gone on his usual round outside the house. The kitchen was empty when he came back to it; but his tobacco-pouch and pipe had been laid on the table, and under them was a scrap of paper torn from the back of a seedsman's catalogue, on which three words were written: 'Don't trouble, Ethan.'

Going into his cold dark 'study' he placed the lantern on the table and, stooping to its light, read the message again and again. It was the first time that Mattie had ever written to him, and the possession of the paper gave him a strange new sense of her nearness; yet it deepened his anguish by reminding him that henceforth they would have no other way of communicating with each other. For the life of her smile, the warmth of her voice, only cold paper and dead words!

Confused motions of rebellion stormed in him. He was too young, too strong, too full of the sap of living, to submit so easily to the destruction of his hopes. Must he wear out all his years at the side of a bitter querulous woman? Other possibilities had been in him, possibilities sacrificed, one by one, to Zeena's narrow-mindedness and ignorance. And what good had come of it? She was a hundred times bitterer and more discontented than when he had married her: the one pleasure left her was to inflict pain on him. All the healthy instincts of self-defence rose up in him against such waste …

He bundled himself into his old coon-skin coat and lay down on the box-sofa to think. Under his cheek he felt a hard object with strange protuberances. It was a cushion which Zeena had made for him when they were engaged – the only piece of needlework he had ever seen her do. He flung it across the floor and propped his head against the wall …

He knew a case of a man over the mountain – a young fellow of about his own age – who had escaped from just such a life of misery by going West with the girl he cared for. His wife had divorced him, and he had married the girl and prospered. Ethan had seen the couple the summer before at Shadd's Falls, where they had come to visit relatives. They had a little girl with fair curls, who wore a gold locket and was dressed like a princess. The deserted wife had not done badly either. Her husband had given her the farm and she had managed to sell it, and with that and the alimony she had started a lunch-room at Bettsbridge and bloomed into activity and importance. Ethan was fired by the thought. Why should he not leave with Mattie the next day, instead of letting her go alone? He would hide his valise under the seat of the sleigh, and Zeena would suspect nothing till she went upstairs for her afternoon nap and found a letter on the bed …

His impulses were still near the surface, and he sprang up, re-lit the lantern, and sat down at the table. He rummaged in the drawer for a sheet of paper, found one, and began to write.

'Zeena, I've done all I could for you, and I don't see as it's been any use. I don't blame you, nor I don't blame myself. Maybe both of us will do better separate. I'm going to try my luck West, and you can sell the farm and mill, and keep the money —'

His pen paused on the word, which brought home to him the relentless conditions of his lot. If he gave the farm and mill to Zeena what would be left him to start his own life with? Once in the West he was sure of picking up work – he would not have feared to try his chance alone. But with Mattie depending on him the case was different. And what of Zeena's fate? Farm and mill were mortgaged to the limit of their value, and even if she found a purchaser – in itself an unlikely chance – it was doubtful if she could clear a thousand dollars on the sale. Meanwhile, how could she keep the farm going? It was only by incessant labour and personal supervision that Ethan drew a meagre living from his land, and his wife, even if she were in better health than she imagined, could never carry such a burden alone.

Well, she could go back to her people, then, and see what they would do for her. It was the fate she was forcing on Mattie – why not let her try it herself? By the time she had discovered his whereabouts, and brought suit for divorce, he would probably – wherever he was – be earning enough to pay her a sufficient alimony. And the alternative was to let Mattie go forth alone, with far less hope of ultimate provision …

He had scattered the contents of the table-drawer in his search for a sheet of paper, and as he took up his pen his eye fell on an old copy of the *Bettsbridge Eagle*. The advertising sheet was folded uppermost, and he read the seductive words: 'Trips to the West: Reduced Rates'.

He drew the lantern nearer and eagerly scanned the fares; then the paper fell from his hand and he pushed aside his unfinished letter. A moment ago he had wondered what he and Mattie were to live on when they reached the West; now he saw that he had not even the money to take her there. Borrowing was out of the question: six months before he had given his only security to raise funds for necessary repairs to the mill, and he knew that without security no one at Starkfield would lend him ten dollars. The inexorable facts closed in on him like prison-warders handcuffing a convict. There was no way out – none. He was a prisoner for life, and now his one ray of light was to be extinguished.

He crept back heavily to the sofa, stretching himself out with limbs so leaden that he felt as if they would never move again. Tears rose in his throat and slowly burned their way to his lids.

As he lay there, the window-pane that faced him, growing gradually lighter, inlaid upon the darkness a square of moon-suffused sky. A crooked tree-branch crossed it, a branch of the apple-tree under which, on summer evenings, he had sometimes found Mattie sitting when he came up from the mill. Slowly the rim of the rainy vapours caught fire and burnt away, and a pure moon swung into the blue. Ethan, rising on his elbow, watched the landscape whiten and shape itself under the sculpture of the moon. This was the night on which he was to have taken Mattie coasting, and there hung the lamp to light them! He looked out at the slopes bathed in lustre, the silver-edged darkness of the woods, the spectral purple of the hills against the sky, and it seemed as though all the beauty of the night had been poured out to mock his wretchedness ...

He fell asleep, and when he woke the chill of the winter dawn was in the room. He felt cold and stiff and hungry, and ashamed of being hungry. He rubbed his eyes and went to the window. A red sun stood over the grey rim of the fields, behind trees that looked black and brittle. He said to himself:

'This is Matt's last day,' and tried to think what the place would be without her.

As he stood there he heard a step behind him and she entered.

'Oh, Ethan – were you here all night?'

She looked so small and pinched, in her poor dress, with the red scarf wound about her, and the cold light turning her paleness sallow, that Ethan stood before her without speaking.

'You must be frozen,' she went on, fixing lustreless eyes on him.

He drew a step nearer. 'How did you know I was here?'

'Because I heard you go down stairs again after I went to bed, and I listened all night, and you didn't come up.'

All his tenderness rushed to his lips. He looked at her and said: 'I'll come right along and make up the kitchen fire.'

They went back to the kitchen, and he fetched the coal and kindlings and cleared out the stove for her, while she brought in the milk and the cold remains of the meat-pie. When warmth began to radiate from the stove, and the first ray of sunlight lay on the kitchen floor, Ethan's dark thoughts melted in the mellower air. The sight of Mattie going about her work as he had seen her on so many mornings made it seem impossible that she should ever cease to be a part of the scene. He said to himself that he had doubtless exaggerated the significance of Zeena's threats, and that she too, with the return of daylight, would come to a saner mood.

He went up to Mattie as she bent above the stove, and laid his hand on her arm. 'I don't want you should trouble either,' he said, looking down into her eyes with a smile.

She flushed up warmly and whispered back: 'No, Ethan, I ain't going to trouble.'

'I guess things'll straighten out,' he added.

There was no answer but a quick throb of her lids, and he went on: 'She ain't said anything this morning?'

'No. I haven't seen her yet.'

'Don't you take any notice when you do.'

With this injunction he left her and went out to the cow-barn. He saw Jotham Powell walking up the hill through the morning mist, and the familiar sight added to his growing conviction of security.

As the two men were clearing out the stalls Jotham rested on his pitch-fork to say: 'Dan'l Byrne's goin' over to the Flats to-day noon, an' he c'd take Mattie's trunk along, and make it easier ridin' when I take her over in the sleigh.'

Ethan looked at him blankly, and he continued: 'Mis' Frome said the new girl'd be at the Flats at five, and I was to take Mattie then, so's 't she could ketch the six o'clock train for Stamford.'

Ethan felt the blood drumming in his temples. He had to wait a moment before he could find voice to say: 'Oh, it ain't so sure about Mattie's going — '

'That so?' said Jotham indifferently; and they went on with their work.

When they returned to the kitchen the two women were already at breakfast. Zeena had an air of unusual alertness and activity. She drank two cups of coffee and fed the cat with the scraps left in the pie-dish; then she rose from her seat and, walking over to the window, snipped two or three yellow leaves from the geraniums. 'Aunt Martha's ain't got a faded leaf on 'em; but they pine away when they ain't cared for,' she said reflectively. Then she turned to Jotham and asked: 'What time'd you say Dan'l Byrne'd be along?'

The hired man threw a hesitating glance at Ethan. 'Round about noon,' he said.

Zeena turned to Mattie. 'That trunk of yours is too heavy for the sleigh, and Dan'l Byrne'll be round to take it over to the Flats,' she said.

'I'm much obliged to you, Zeena,' said Mattie.

'I'd like to go over things with you first,' Zeena continued in an unperturbed voice. 'I know there's a huckabuck towel⁰ missing; and I can't take out what you done with that match-safe⁰ 't used to stand behind the stuffed owl in the parlour.'

She went out, followed by Mattie, and when the men were alone Jotham said to his employer: 'I guess I better let Dan'l come round, then.'

Ethan finished his usual morning tasks about the house and barn; then he said to Jotham: 'I'm going down to Starkfield. Tell them not to wait dinner.'

The passion of rebellion had broken out in him again. That which had seemed incredible in the sober light of day had really come to pass, and he was to assist as a helpless spectator at Mattie's banishment. His manhood was humbled by the part he was compelled to play and by the thought of what Mattie must think of him. Confused impulses struggled in him as he strode along to the village. He had made up his mind to do something, but he did not know what it would be.

The early mist had vanished and the fields lay like a silver shield under the sun. It was one of the days when the glitter of winter shines through a pale haze of spring. Every yard of the road was alive with Mattie's presence, and there was hardly a branch against the sky or a tangle of brambles on the bank in which some bright shred of memory was not caught. Once, in the stillness, the call of a bird in a mountain ash was so like her laughter that his heart tightened and then grew large; and all these things made him see that something must be done at once.

Suddenly it occurred to him that Andrew Hale, who was a kind-hearted man, might be induced to reconsider his refusal and advance a small sum of lumber if he were told that Zeena's ill-health made it necessary to hire a servant. Hale, after all, knew enough of Ethan's situation to make it possible for the latter to renew his appeal without too much loss of pride; and, moreover, how much did pride count in the ebullition of passions in his breast?

The more he considered his plan the more hopeful it seemed. If he could get Mrs Hale's ear he felt certain of success, and with fifty dollars in his pocket nothing could keep him from Mattie …

His first object was to reach Starkfield before Hale had started for his work; he knew the carpenter had a job down the Corbury road and was likely to leave his house early. Ethan's long strides grew more rapid with the accelerated beat of his thoughts, and as he reached the foot of School House Hill he caught sight of Hale's sleigh in the distance. He hurried forward to meet it, but as it drew nearer he saw that it was driven by the carpenter's youngest boy and that the figure at his side, looking like a large upright cocoon in spectacles, was that of Mrs Hale. Ethan signed to them to stop, and Mrs Hale leaned forward, her pink wrinkles twinkling with benevolence.

'Mr Hale? Why, yes, you'll find him down home now. He ain't going to his work this forenoon. He woke up with a touch o' lumbago, and I just made him put on one of old Dr Kidder's plasters and set right up into the fire.'

Beaming maternally on Ethan, she bent over to add: 'I on'y just heard from Mr Hale 'bout Zeena's going over to Bettsbridge to see that new doctor. I'm real sorry she's feeling so bad again! I hope he thinks he can do something for her. I don't know anybody round here's had more sickness than Zeena. I always tell Mr Hale I don't know what she'd 'a' done if she hadn't 'a' had you to look after her; and I used to say the same thing 'bout your mother. You've had an awful mean time, Ethan Frome.'

She gave him a last nod of sympathy while her son chirped to the horse; and Ethan, as she drove off, stood in the middle of the road and stared after the retreating sleigh.

It was a long time since any one had spoken to him as kindly as Mrs Hale. Most people were either indifferent to his troubles, or disposed to think it natural that a young fellow of his age should have carried without repining the burden of three crippled lives. But Mrs Hale had said, 'You've had an awful mean time, Ethan Frome,' and he felt less alone with his misery. If the Hales were sorry for him they would surely respond to his appeal ...

He started down the road toward their house, but at the end of a few yards he pulled up sharply, the blood in his face. For the first time, in the light of the words he had just heard, he saw what he was about to do. He was planning to take advantage of the Hales' sympathy to obtain money from them on false pretences. That was a plain statement of the cloudy purpose which had driven him in headlong to Starkfield.

With the sudden perception of the point to which his madness had carried him, the madness fell and he saw his life before him as it was. He was a poor man, the husband of a sickly woman, whom his desertion would leave alone and destitute; and even if he had had the heart to desert her he could have done so only by deceiving two kindly people who had pitied him.

He turned and walked slowly back to the farm.

Chapter 9

At the kitchen door Daniel Byrne sat in his sleigh behind a big-boned grey who pawed the snow and swung his long head restlessly from side to side.

Ethan went into the kitchen and found his wife by the stove. Her head was wrapped in her shawl, and she was reading a book called 'Kidney Troubles and Their Cure' on which he had had to pay extra postage only a few days before.

Zeena did not move or look up when he entered, and after a moment he asked: 'Where's Mattie?'

Without lifting her eyes from the page she replied: 'I presume she's getting down her trunk.'

The blood rushed to his face. 'Getting down her trunk – alone?'

'Jotham Powell's down in the wood-lot, and Dan'l Byrne says he dasn't leave that horse,' she returned.

Her husband, without stopping to hear the end of the phrase, had left the kitchen and sprung up the stairs. The door of Mattie's room was shut, and he wavered a moment on the landing. 'Matt,' he said in a low voice; but there was no answer, and he put his hand on the door-knob.

He had never been in her room except once, in the early summer, when he had gone there to plaster up a leak in the eaves, but he remembered exactly how everything had looked: the red-and-white quilt on her narrow bed, the pretty pin-cushion on the chest of drawers, and over it the enlarged photograph of her mother, in an oxydized frame, with a bunch of dyed grasses at the back. Now these and all other tokens of her presence had vanished and the room looked as bare and comfortless as when Zeena had shown her into it on the day of her arrival. In the middle of the floor stood her trunk, and on the trunk she sat in her Sunday dress, her back turned to the door and her face in her hands. She had not heard Ethan's call because she was sobbing and she did not hear his step till he stood close behind her and laid his hands on her shoulders.

'Matt – oh, don't – oh, *Matt!*'

She started up, lifting her wet face to his. 'Ethan – I thought I wasn't ever going to see you again!'

He took her in his arms, pressing her close, and with a trembling hand smoothed away the hair from her forehead.

'Not see me again? What do you mean?'

She sobbed out: 'Jotham said you told him we wasn't to wait dinner for you, and I thought — '

'You thought I meant to cut it?' he finished for her grimly.

She clung to him without answering, and he laid his lips on her hair, which was soft yet springy, like certain mosses on warm slopes, and had the faint woody fragrance of fresh sawdust in the sun.

Through the door they heard Zeena's voice calling out from below: 'Dan'l Byrne says you better hurry up if you want him to take that trunk.'

They drew apart with stricken faces. Words of resistance rushed to Ethan's lips and died there. Mattie found her handkerchief and dried her eyes; then, bending down, she took hold of a handle of the trunk.

Ethan put her aside. 'You let go, Matt,' he ordered her.

She answered: 'It takes two to coax it round the corner;' and submitting to this argument he grasped the other handle, and together they manoeuvred the heavy trunk out to the landing.

'Now let go,' he repeated; then he shouldered the trunk and carried it down the stairs and across the passage to the kitchen. Zeena, who had gone back to her seat by the stove, did not lift her head from her book as he passed. Mattie followed him out of the door and helped him to lift the trunk into the back of the sleigh. When it was in place they stood side by side on the door-step, watching Daniel Byrne plunge off behind his fidgety horse.

It seemed to Ethan that his heart was bound with cords which an unseen hand was tightening with every tick of the clock. Twice he opened his lips to speak to Mattie and found no breath. At length, as she turned to re-enter the house, he laid a detaining hand on her.

'I'm going to drive you over, Matt,' he whispered.

She murmured back: 'I think Zeena wants I should go with Jotham.'

'I'm going to drive you over,' he repeated; and she went into the kitchen without answering.

At dinner Ethan could not eat. If he lifted his eyes they rested on Zeena's pinched face, and the corners of her straight lips seemed to quiver away into a smile. She ate well, declaring that the mild weather made her feel better, and pressed a second helping of beans on Jotham Powell, whose wants she generally ignored.

Mattie, when the meal was over, went about her usual task of clearing the table and washing up the dishes. Zeena, after feeding the cat, had returned to her rocking-chair by the stove, and Jotham Powell, who always lingered last, reluctantly pushed back his chair and moved toward the door.

On the threshold he turned back to say to Ethan: 'What time'll I come round for Mattie?'

Ethan was standing near the window, mechanically filling his pipe while he watched Mattie move to and fro. He answered: 'You needn't come round; I'm going to drive her over myself.'

He saw the rise of the colour in Mattie's averted cheek, and the quick lifting of Zeena's head.

'I want you should stay here this afternoon, Ethan,' his wife said. 'Jotham can drive Mattie over.'

Mattie flung an imploring glance at him, but he repeated curtly: 'I'm going to drive her over myself.'

Zeena continued in the same even tone: 'I wanted you should stay and fix up that stove in Mattie's room afore the girl gets here. It ain't been drawing right for nigh on a month now.'

Ethan's voice rose indignantly. 'If it was good enough for Mattie I guess it's good enough for a hired girl.'

'That girl that's coming told me she was used to a house where they had a furnace,' Zeena persisted with the same monotonous mildness.

'She'd better ha' stayed there then,' he flung back at her; and turning to Mattie he added in a hard voice: 'You be ready by three, Matt; I've got business at Corbury.'

Jotham Powell had started for the barn, and Ethan strode down after him aflame with anger. The pulses in his temples throbbed and a fog was in his eyes. He went about his task without knowing what force directed him, or whose hands and feet were fulfilling its orders. It was not till he led out the sorrel and backed him between the shafts of the sleigh that he once more became conscious of what he was doing. As he passed the bridle over the horse's head, and wound the traces around the shafts, he remembered the day when he had made the same preparations in order to drive over and meet his wife's cousin at the Flats. It was little more than a year ago, on just such a soft afternoon, with a 'feel' of spring in the air. The sorrel, turning the same big ringed eye on him, nuzzled the palm of his hand in the same way; and one by one all the days between rose up and stood before him ...

He flung the bearskin into the sleigh, climbed to the seat, and drove up to the house. When he entered the kitchen it was empty, but Mattie's bag and shawl lay ready by the door. He went to the foot of the stairs and listened. No sound reached him from above, but presently he thought he heard someone moving about in his deserted study, and pushing open the door he saw Mattie, in her hat and jacket, standing with her back to him near the table.

She started at his approach and turning quickly, said: 'Is it time?'

'What are you doing here, Matt?' he asked her.

She looked at him timidly. 'I was just taking a look round – that's all,' she answered, with a wavering smile.

They went back into the kitchen without speaking, and Ethan picked up her bag and shawl.

'Where's Zeena?' he asked.

'She went upstairs right after dinner. She said she had those shooting pains again, and didn't want to be disturbed.'

'Didn't she say good-bye to you?'

'No. That was all she said.'

Ethan, looking slowly about the kitchen, said to himself with a shudder that in a few hours he would be returning to it alone. Then the sense of unreality overcame him once more, and he could not bring himself to believe that Mattie stood there for the last time before him.

'Come on,' he said almost gaily, opening the door and putting her bag into the sleigh. He sprang to his seat and bent over to tuck the rug about her as she slipped into the place at his side. 'Now then, go 'long,' he said, with a shake of the reins that sent the sorrel placidly jogging down the hill.

'We got lots of time for a good ride, Matt!' he cried, seeking her hand beneath the fur and pressing it in his. His face tingled and he felt dizzy, as if he had stopped in at the Starkfield saloon on a zero day for a drink.

At the gate, instead of making for Starkfield, he turned the sorrel to the right, up the Bettsbridge road. Mattie sat silent, giving no sign of surprise; but after a moment she said: 'Are you going round by Shadow Pond?'

He laughed and answered: 'I knew you'd know!'

She drew closer under the bearskin, so that, looking sideways around his coat-sleeve, he could just catch the tip of her nose and a blown brown wave of hair. They drove slowly up the road between fields glistening under the pale sun, and then bent to the right down a lane edged with spruce and larch. Ahead of them, a long way off, a range of hills stained by mottlings of black forest flowed away in round white curves against the sky. The lane passed into a pine-wood with boles reddening in the afternoon sun and delicate blue shadows on the snow. As they entered it the breeze fell and a warm stillness seemed to drop from the branches with the dropping needles. Here the snow was so pure that the tiny tracks of wood-animals had left on it intricate lace-like patterns, and the bluish cones caught in its surface stood out like ornaments of bronze.

Ethan drove on in silence till they reached a part of the wood where the pines were more widely spaced, then he drew up and helped Mattie to get out of the sleigh. They passed between the aromatic trunks, the snow breaking crisply under their feet, till they came to a small sheet of water with steep wooded sides. Across its frozen surface, from the farther bank, a single hill rising against the western sun threw the long conical shadow which gave the lake its name. It was a shy secret spot, full of the same dumb melancholy that Ethan felt in his heart.

He looked up and down the little pebbly beach till his eye lit on a fallen tree-trunk half submerged in snow.

'There's where we sat at the picnic,' he reminded her.

The entertainment of which he spoke was one of the few that they had taken part in together: a 'church picnic' which, on a long afternoon of the preceding summer, had filled the retired place with merry-making. Mattie had begged him to go with her but he had refused. Then, toward sunset, coming down from the mountain where he had been felling timber, he had been caught by some strayed revellers and drawn into the group by the lake, where Mattie, encircled by facetious youths, and bright as a blackberry under her spreading hat, was brewing coffee over a gipsy fire. He remembered the shyness he had felt at approaching her in his uncouth clothes, and then the lighting up of her face, and the way she had broken through the group to come to him with a cup in her hand. They had sat for a few minutes on the fallen log by the pond, and she had missed her gold locket, and set the young men searching for it; and it was Ethan who had spied it in the moss ... That was all; but all their intercourse had been made up of just such inarticulate flashes, when they seemed to come suddenly upon happiness as if they had surprised a butterfly in the winter woods ...

'It was right there I found your locket,' he said, pushing his foot into a dense tuft of blueberry bushes.

'I never saw anybody with such sharp eyes!' she answered.

She sat down on the tree-trunk in the sun and he sat down beside her.

'You were as pretty as a picture in that pink hat,' he said.

She laughed with pleasure. 'Oh, I guess it was the hat!' she rejoined.

They had never before avowed their inclination so openly, and Ethan, for a moment, had the illusion that he was a free man, wooing the girl he meant to marry. He looked at her hair and longed to touch it again, and to tell her that it smelt of the woods; but he had never learned to say such things.

Suddenly she rose to her feet and said: 'We mustn't stay here any longer.'

He continued to gaze at her vaguely, only half-roused from his dream. 'There's plenty of time,' he answered.

They stood looking at each other as if the eyes of each were straining to absorb and hold fast the other's image. There were things he had to say to her before they parted, but he could not say them in that place of summer memories, and he turned and followed her in silence to the sleigh. As they drove away the sun sank behind the hill and the pine-boles turned from red to grey.

By a devious track between the fields they wound back to the Starkfield road. Under the open sky the light was still clear, with a reflection of cold red on the eastern hills. The clumps of trees in the snow seemed to draw together in ruffled lumps, like birds with their heads under their wings; and the sky, as it paled, rose higher, leaving the earth more alone.

As they turned into the Starkfield road Ethan said: 'Matt, what do you mean to do?'

She did not answer at once, but at length she said: 'I'll try to get a place in a store.'

'You know you can't do it. The bad air and the standing all day nearly killed you before.'

'I'm a lot stronger than I was before I came to Starkfield.'

'And now you're going to throw away all the good it's done you!'

There seemed to be no answer to this, and again they drove on for a while without speaking. With every yard of the way some spot where they had stood, and laughed together or been silent, clutched at Ethan and dragged him back.

'Isn't there any of your father's folks could help you?'

'There isn't any of 'em I'd ask.'

He lowered his voice to say: 'You know there's nothing I wouldn't do for you if I could.'

'I know there isn't.'

'But I can't — '

She was silent, but he felt a slight tremor in the shoulder against his.

'Oh, Matt,' he broke out, 'if I could ha' gone with you now I'd ha' done it — '

She turned to him, pulling a scrap of paper from her breast. 'Ethan – I found this,' she stammered. Even in the failing light he saw it was the letter to his wife that he had begun the night before and forgotten to destroy. Through his astonishment there ran a fierce thrill of joy. 'Matt — ' he cried; 'if I could ha' done it, would you?'

'Oh, Ethan, Ethan – what's the use?' With a sudden movement she tore the letter in shreds and sent them fluttering off into the snow.

'Tell me, Matt! Tell me!' he adjured her.

She was silent for a moment; then she said, in such a low tone that he had to stoop his head to hear her: 'I used to think of it sometimes, summer nights, when the moon was so bright I couldn't sleep.'

His heart reeled with the sweetness of it. 'As long ago as that?'

She answered, as if the date had long been fixed for her: 'The first time was at Shadow Pond.'

'Was that why you gave me my coffee before the others?'

'I don't know. Did I? I was dreadfully put out when you wouldn't go to the picnic with me; and then, when I saw you coming down the road, I thought maybe you'd gone home that way o' purpose; and that made me glad.'

They were silent again. They had reached the point where the road dipped to the hollow by Ethan's mill and as they descended the darkness descended with them, dropping down like a black veil from the heavy hemlock boughs.

'I'm tied hand and foot, Matt. There isn't a thing I can do,' he began again.

'You must write to me sometimes, Ethan.'

'Oh, what good'll writing do? I want to put my hand out and touch you. I want to do for you and care for you. I want to be there when you're sick and when you're lonesome.'

'You mustn't think but what I'll do all right.'

'You won't need me, you mean? I suppose you'll marry!'

'Oh, Ethan!' she cried.

'I don't know how it is you make me feel, Matt. I'd a'most rather have you dead than that!'

'Oh, I wish I was, I wish I was!' she sobbed.

The sound of her weeping shook him out of his dark anger, and he felt ashamed.

'Don't let's talk that way,' he whispered.

'Why shouldn't we, when it's true? I've been wishing it every minute of the day.'

'Matt! You be quiet! Don't you say it.'

'There's never anybody been good to me but you.'

'Don't say that either, when I can't lift a hand for you!'

'Yes; but it's true just the same.'

They had reached the top of School House Hill and Starkfield lay below them in the twilight. A cutter, mounting the road from the village, passed them by in a joyous flutter of bells, and they straightened themselves and looked ahead with rigid faces. Along the main street lights had begun to shine from the house-fronts and stray figures were turning in here and there at the gates. Ethan, with a touch of his whip, roused the sorrel to a languid trot.

As they drew near the end of the village the cries of children reached them, and they saw a knot of boys, with sleds behind them, scattering across the open space before the church.

'I guess this'll be their last coast for a day or two,' Ethan said, looking up at the mild sky.

Mattie was silent, and he added: 'We were to have gone down last night.'

Still she did not speak and, prompted by an obscure desire to help himself and her through their miserable last hour, he went on discursively: 'Ain't it funny we haven't been down together but just that once last winter?'

She answered: 'It wasn't often I got down to the village.'

'That's so,' he said.

They had reached the crest of the Corbury road, and between the indistinct white glimmer of the church and the black curtain of the Varnum spruces the slope stretched away below them without a sled on its length. Some erratic impulse prompted Ethan to say: 'How'd you like me to take you down now?'

She forced a laugh. 'Why, there isn't time!'

'There's all the time we want. Come along!' His one desire now was to postpone the moment of turning the sorrel toward the Flats.

'But the girl,' she faltered. 'The girl'll be waiting at the station.'

'Well, let her wait. You'd have to if she didn't. Come!'

The note of authority in his voice seemed to subdue her, and when he had jumped from the sleigh he let him help her out, saying only, with a vague feint of reluctance: 'But there isn't a sled round anywheres.'

'Yes, there is! Right over there under the spruces.'

He threw the bearskin over the sorrel, who stood passively by the roadside, hanging a meditative head. Then he caught Mattie's hand and drew her after him toward the sled.

She seated herself obediently and he took his place behind her, so close that her hair brushed his face. 'All right, Matt?' he called out, as if the width of the road had been between them.

She turned her head to say: 'It's dreadfully dark. Are you sure you can see?'

He laughed contemptuously: 'I could go down this coast with my eyes tied!' and she laughed with him, as if she liked his audacity. Nevertheless he sat still a moment, straining his eyes down the long hill, for it was the most confusing hour of the evening, the hour when the last clearness from the upper sky is merged with the rising night in a blur that disguises landmarks and falsifies distances.

'Now!' he cried.

The sled started with a bound, and they flew on through the dusk, gathering smoothness and speed as they went, with the hollow night opening out below them and the air singing by like an organ. Mattie sat perfectly still, but as they reached the bend at the foot of the hill, where the big elm thrust out a deadly elbow, he fancied that she shrank a little closer.

'Don't be scared, Matt!' he cried exultantly, as they spun safely past it and flew down the second slope; and when they reached the level ground beyond, and the speed of the sled began to slacken, he heard her give a little laugh of glee.

They sprang off and started to walk back up the hill. Ethan dragged the sled with one hand and passed the other through Mattie's arm.

'Were you scared I'd run you into the elm?' he asked with a boyish laugh.

'I told you I was never scared with you,' she answered.

The strange exaltation of his mood had brought on one of his rare fits of boastfulness. 'It *is* a tricky place, though. The least swerve, and we'd never ha' come up again. But I can measure distances to a hair's-breadth – always could.'

She murmured: 'I always say you've got the surest eye ...'

Deep silence had fallen with the starless dusk, and they leaned on each other without speaking; but at every step of their climb Ethan said to himself: 'It's the last time we'll ever walk together.'

They mounted slowly to the top of the hill. When they were abreast of the church he stooped his head to her to ask: 'Are you tired?' and she answered, breathing quickly: 'It was splendid!'

With a pressure of his arm he guided her toward the Norway spruces. 'I guess this sled must be Ned Hale's. Anyhow I'll leave it where I found it.' He drew the sled up to the Varnum gate and rested it against the fence. As he raised himself he suddenly felt Mattie close to him among the shadows.

'Is this where Ned and Ruth kissed each other?' she whispered breathlessly, and flung her arms about him. Her lips, groping for his, swept over his face, and he held her fast in a rapture of surprise.

'Good-bye – good-bye,' she stammered, and kissed him again.

'Oh, Matt, I can't let you go!' broke from him in the same old cry.

She freed herself from his hold and he heard her sobbing. 'Oh, I can't go either!' she wailed.

'Matt! What'll we do? What'll we do?'

They clung to each other's hands like children, and her body shook with desperate sobs.

Through the stillness they heard the church clock striking five.

'Oh, Ethan, it's time!' she cried.

He drew her back to him. 'Time for what? You don't suppose I'm going to leave you now?'

'If I missed my train where'd I go?'

'Where are you going if you catch it?'

She stood silent, her hands lying cold and relaxed in his.

'What's the good of either of us going anywheres without the other one now?' he said.

She remained motionless, as if she had not heard him. Then she snatched her hands from his, threw her arms about his neck, and pressed a sudden drenched cheek against his face. 'Ethan! Ethan! I want you to take me down again!'

'Down where?'

'The coast. Right off,' she panted. 'So 't we'll never come up any more.'

'Matt! What on earth do you mean?'

She put her lips close against his ear to say: 'Right into the big elm. You said you could. So 't we'd never have to leave each other any more.'

'Why, what are you talking of? You're crazy!'

'I'm not crazy; but I will be if I leave you.'

'Oh, Matt, Matt — ' he groaned.

She tightened her fierce hold about his neck. Her face lay close to his face.

'Ethan, where'll I go if I leave you? I don't know how to get along alone. You said so yourself just now. Nobody but you was ever good to me. And there'll be that strange girl in the house ... and she'll sleep in my bed, where I used to lay nights and listen to hear you come up the stairs ... '

The words were like fragments torn from his heart. With them came the hated vision of the house he was going back to – of the stairs he would have to go up every night, of the woman who would wait for him there. And the sweetness of Mattie's avowal, the wild wonder of knowing at last that all that had happened to him had happened to her too, made the other vision more abhorrent, the other life more intolerable to return to ...

Her pleadings still came to him between short sobs, but he no longer heard what she was saying. Her hat had slipped back and he was stroking her hair. He wanted to get the feeling of it into his hand, so that it would sleep there like a seed in winter. Once he found her mouth again, and they seemed to be by the pond together in the burning August sun. But his cheek touched hers, and it was cold and full of weeping, and he saw the road to the Flats under the night and heard the whistle of the train up the line.

The spruces swathed them in blackness and silence. They might have been in their coffins underground. He said to himself: 'Perhaps it'll feel like this ... ' and then again: 'After this I sha'n't feel anything ... '

Suddenly he heard the old sorrel whinny across the road, and thought: 'He's wondering why he doesn't get his supper ...'

'Come,' Mattie whispered, tugging at his hand.

Her sombre violence constrained him: she seemed the embodied instrument of fate. He pulled the sled out, blinking like a night-bird as he passed from the shade of the spruces into the transparent dusk of the open. The slope below them was deserted. All Starkfield was at supper, and not a figure crossed the open space before the church. The sky, swollen with the clouds that announce a thaw, hung as low as before a summer storm. He strained his eyes through the dimness, and they seemed less keen, less capable than usual.

He took his seat on the sled and Mattie instantly placed herself in front of him. Her hat had fallen into the snow and his lips were in her hair. He stretched out his legs, drove his heels into the road to keep the sled from slipping forward, and bent her head back between his hands. Then suddenly he sprang up again.

'Get up,' he ordered her.

It was the tone she always heeded, but she cowered down in her seat, repeating vehemently: 'No, no, no!'

'Get up!'

'Why?'

'I want to sit in front.'

'No, no! How can you steer in front?'

'I don't have to. We'll follow the track.'

They spoke in smothered whispers, as though the night were listening.

'Get up! Get up!' he urged her; but she kept on repeating: 'Why do you want to sit in front?'

'Because I – because I want to feel you holding me,' he stammered, and dragged her to her feet.

The answer seemed to satisfy her, or else she yielded to the power of his voice. He bent down, feeling in the obscurity for the glassy slide worn by preceding coasters, and placed the runners carefully between its edges. She waited while he seated himself with crossed legs in the front of the sled; then she crouched quickly down at his back and clasped her arms about him. Her breath in his neck set him shuddering again, and he almost sprang from his seat. But in a flash he remembered the alternative. She was right: this was better than parting. He leaned back and drew her mouth to his ...

Just as they started he heard the sorrel's whinny again, and the familiar wistful call, and all the confused images it brought with it, went with him down the first reach of the road. Half-way down there was a sudden drop, then a rise, and after that another long delirious descent. As they took wing for this it seemed to him that they were flying indeed, flying far up into the cloudy night, with Starkfield immeasurably below them, falling away like a speck in space ... Then the big elm shot up ahead, lying in wait for them at the bend of the road, and he said between his teeth: 'We can fetch it; I know we can fetch it — '

As they flew toward the tree Mattie pressed her arms tighter, and her blood seemed to be in his veins. Once or twice the sled swerved a little under them. He slanted his body to keep it headed for the elm, repeating to himself again and again: 'I know we can fetch it;' and little phrases she had spoken ran through his head and danced before him on the air. The big tree loomed bigger and closer, and as they bore down on it he thought: 'It's waiting for us: it seems to know.' But suddenly his wife's face, with twisted monstrous lineaments, thrust itself between him and his goal, and he made an instinctive movement to brush it aside. The sled swerved in response, but he righted it again, kept it straight, and drove down on the black projecting mass. There was a last instant when the air shot past him like millions of fiery wires; and then the elm ...

The sky was still thick, but looking straight up he saw a single star, and tried vaguely to reckon whether it was Sirius, or – or – The effort tired him too much, and he closed his heavy lids and thought that he would sleep ... The stillness was so profound that he heard a little animal twittering somewhere near by under the snow. It made a small frightened *cheep* like a field mouse, and he wondered languidly if it were hurt. Then he understood that it must be in pain: pain so excruciating that he seemed, mysteriously, to feel it shooting through his own body. He tried in vain to roll over in the direction of the sound, and stretched his left arm out across the snow. And now it was as though he felt rather than heard the twittering; it seemed to be under his palm, which rested on something soft and springy. The thought of the animal's suffering was intolerable to him and he struggled to raise himself, and could not because a rock, or some huge mass, seemed to be lying on him. But he continued to finger about cautiously with his left hand, thinking he might get hold of the little creature and help it; and all at once he knew that the soft thing he had touched was Mattie's hair and that his hand was on her face.

He dragged himself to his knees, the monstrous load on him moving with him as he moved, and his hand went over and over her face, and he felt that the twittering came from her lips …

He got his face down close to hers, with his ear to her mouth, and in the darkness he saw her eyes open and heard her say his name.

'Oh, Matt, I thought we'd fetched it,' he moaned; and far off, up the hill, he heard the sorrel whinny, and thought: 'I ought to be getting him his feed … ' … … … … … … … … … …
… …
… …

The querulous drone ceased as I entered Frome's kitchen, and of the two women sitting there I could not tell which had been the speaker.

One of them, on my appearing, raised her tall bony figure from her seat, not as if to welcome me – for she threw me no more than a brief glance of surprise – but simply to set about preparing the meal which Frome's absence had delayed. A slatternly calico wrapper hung from her shoulders and the wisps of her thin grey hair were drawn away from a high forehead and fastened at the back by a broken comb. She had pale opaque eyes which revealed nothing and reflected nothing, and her narrow lips were of the same sallow colour as her face.

The other woman was much smaller and slighter. She sat huddled in an arm-chair near the stove, and when I came in she turned her head quickly toward me, without the least corresponding movement of her body. Her hair was as grey as her companion's, her face as bloodless and shrivelled, but amber-tinted, with swarthy shadows sharpening the nose and hollowing the temples. Under her shapeless dress her body kept its limp immobility, and her dark eyes had the bright witch-like stare that disease of the spine sometimes gives.

Even for that part of the country the kitchen was a poor-looking place. With the exception of the dark-eyed woman's chair, which looked like a soiled relic of luxury bought at a country auction, the furniture was of the roughest kind. Three coarse china plates and a broken-nosed milk-jug had been set on a greasy table scored with knife-cuts, and a couple of straw-bottomed chairs and a kitchen dresser of unpainted pine stood meagrely against the plaster walls.

'My, it's cold here! The fire must be 'most out,' Frome said, glancing about him apologetically as he followed me in.

The tall woman, who had moved away from us toward the dresser, took no notice; but the other, from her cushioned niche, answered complainingly, in a high thin voice: 'It's on'y just been made up this very minute. Zeena fell asleep and slep' ever so long, and I thought I'd be frozen stiff before I could wake her up and get her to 'tend to it.'

I knew then that it was she who had been speaking when we entered.

Her companion, who was just coming back to the table with the remains of a cold mince-pie in a battered pie-dish, set down her unappetising burden without appearing to hear the accusation brought against her.

Frome stood hesitatingly before her as she advanced; then he looked at me and said: 'This is my wife, Mis' Frome.' After another interval he added, turning toward the figure in the arm-chair: 'And this is Miss Mattie Silver ... '

Mrs Hale, tender soul, had pictured me as lost in the Flats and buried under a snow-drift; and so lively was her satisfaction on seeing me safely restored to her the next morning that I felt my peril had caused me to advance several degrees in her favour.

Great was her amazement, and that of old Mrs Varnum, on learning that Ethan Frome's old horse had carried me to and from Corbury Junction through the worst blizzard of the winter; greater still their surprise when they heard that his master had taken me in for the night.

Beneath their wondering exclamations I felt a secret curiosity to know what impressions I had received from my night in the Frome household, and divined that the best way of breaking down their reserve was to let them try to penetrate mine. I therefore confined myself to saying, in a matter-of-fact tone, that I had been received with great kindness, and that

Frome had made a bed for me in a room on the ground floor which seemed in happier days to have been fitted up as a kind of writing-room or study.

'Well,' Mrs Hale mused, 'in such a storm I suppose he felt he couldn't do less than take you in – but I guess it went hard with Ethan. I don't believe but what you're the only stranger has set foot in that house for over twenty years. He's that proud he don't even like his oldest friends to go there; and I don't know as any do, any more, except myself and the doctor ... '

'You still go there, Mrs Hale?' I ventured.

'I used to go a good deal after the accident, when I was first married; but after awhile I got to think it made 'em feel worse to see us. And then one thing and another came, and my own troubles ... But I generally make out to drive over there round about New Year's, and once in the summer. Only I always try to pick a day when Ethan's off somewheres. It's bad enough to see the two women sitting there – but *his* face, when he looks round that bare place, just kills me ... You see, I can look back and call it up in his mother's day, before their troubles.'

Old Mrs Varnum, by this time, had gone up to bed, and her daughter and I were sitting alone, after supper, in the austere seclusion of the horse-hair parlour. Mrs Hale glanced at me tentatively, as though trying to see how much footing my conjectures gave her; and I guessed that if she had kept silence till now it was because she had been waiting, through all the years, for some one who should see what she alone had seen.

I waited to let her trust in me gather strength before I said: 'Yes, it's pretty bad, seeing all three of them there together.'

She drew her mild brows into a frown of pain. 'It was just awful from the beginning. I was here in the house when they were carried up – they laid Mattie Silver in the room you're in. She and I were great friends, and she was to have been my bridesmaid in the spring ... When she came to I went up to her and stayed all night. They gave her things to quiet her, and she didn't know much till to'rd morning, and then all of a sudden she woke up just like herself, and looked straight at me out of her big eyes, and said … Oh, I don't know why I'm telling you all this,' Mrs Hale broke off, crying.

She took off her spectacles, wiped the moisture from them, and put them on again with an unsteady hand. 'It got about the next day,' she went on, 'that Zeena Frome had sent Mattie off in a hurry because she had a hired girl coming, and the folks here could never rightly tell what she and Ethan were doing that night coasting, when they'd ought to have been on their way to the Flats to ketch the train … I never knew myself what Zeena thought – I don't to this day. Nobody knows Zeena's thoughts. Anyhow, when she heard o' the accident she came right in and stayed with Ethan over to the minister's, where they'd carried him. And as soon as the doctors said that Mattie could be moved, Zeena sent for her and took her back to the farm.'

'And there she's been ever since?'

Mrs Hale answered simply: 'There was nowhere else for her to go;' and my heart tightened at the thought of the hard compulsions of the poor.

'Yes, there she's been,' Mrs Hale continued, 'and Zeena's done for her, and done for Ethan, as good as she could. It was a miracle, considering how sick she was – but she seemed to be raised right up just when the call came to her. Not as she's ever given up doctoring, and she's had sick spells right along; but she's had the strength given her to care for those two for over twenty years, and before the accident came she thought she couldn't even care for herself.'

Mrs Hale paused a moment, and I remained silent, plunged in the vision of what her words evoked. 'It's horrible for them all,' I murmured.

'Yes: it's pretty bad. And they ain't any of 'em easy people either. Mattie *was*, before the accident; I never knew a sweeter nature. But she's suffered too much – that's what I always say when folks tell me how she's soured. And Zeena, she was always cranky. Not but what she bears with Mattie wonderful – I've seen that myself. But sometimes the two of them get going at each other, and then Ethan's face'd break your heart … When I see that, I think it's *him* that suffers most … anyhow it ain't Zeena, because she ain't got the time … It's a pity, though,' Mrs Hale ended, sighing, 'that they're all shut up there'n that one kitchen. In the summertime, on pleasant days, they move Mattie into the parlour, or out in the door-yard, and that makes it easier … but winters there's the fires to be thought of; and there ain't a dime to spare up at the Fromes'.'

Mrs Hale drew a deep breath, as though her memory were eased of its long burden, and she had no more to say; but suddenly an impulse of complete avowal seized her.

She took off her spectacles again, leaned toward me across the bead-work table-cover, and went on with lowered voice: 'There was one day, about a week after the accident, when they all thought Mattie couldn't live. Well, I say it's a pity she *did*. I said it right out to our minister once, and he was shocked at me. Only he wasn't with me that morning when she first came to … And I say, if she'd ha' died, Ethan might ha' lived; and the way they are now, I don't see's there's much difference between the Fromes up at the farm and the Fromes down in the graveyard; 'cept that down there they're all quiet, and the women have got to hold their tongues.'

RESOURCE NOTES

Who has written *Ethan Frome* and why?

Edith Newbold Jones, who used her married name of Wharton throughout her professional career, was born on 24 January 1862 in a fashionable and expensive part of New York City – 14 West 23rd Street, near Madison Square. Her parents were descended from successful English and Dutch American merchants and did not have to work. They were rich enough to take summer vacations in Europe, which Edith loved, and they had a large house in Newport, Massachusetts, then an extremely fashionable seaside resort.

In 1885 she married Teddy Wharton, who was thirteen years older than her, and who as the years passed became increasingly ill. Biographers of Edith Wharton, such as R. W. B. Lewis (1975) and Shari Benstock (1994) have described the way that Edith Wharton's marriage was destroyed by a combination of her husband's ill health and depression, and the way that this in turn led to their unsatisfactory sexual relationship. Just before she wrote *Ethan Frome*, Edith Wharton, now in her forties, had a secret affair with a journalist called Morton Fullerton, and although it was passionate and sexually fulfilling for her, she hated the deceit of having an affair and it was not to last.

Biographers have an interest in interpreting fiction in terms of mirroring life, and the story of Ethan, trapped in a loveless marriage and burning with passion for the younger Mattie is seen as analogous to that of her own marriage, with the roles reversed. In his biography, R. W. B. Lewis says that the names give us a clue – 'Ethan' is a bit like 'Edith' and 'Mattie' is a little like 'Morton'. Zeena, like Edith's husband Teddy Wharton, requires constant nursing.

The problem with this reading is that it doesn't do full justice to the fact that although Edith Wharton made a number of changes to the original version written for her French tutor in Paris, there is still no sexual relationship between Ethan and Mattie in the 1911 version of the story. In fact the narrative goes out of its way to say that there wasn't one.

So although there are clearly parallels between what was happening in Edith Wharton's personal life and the triangular relationship in the novel, the differences are striking enough to discourage the careful reader from saying, 'She wrote this in response to her first really passionate, sexual affair'. There is more to it than this!

Edith Wharton's life took a very unpredictable turn three years after the publication of *Ethan Frome*, as did the lives of millions of others across the world. During the First World War (1914–1918) Edith Wharton became actively involved in war work with orphans and refugees in France, for which she was awarded the Cross of the Légion d'Honneur in 1915. After the war she continued to live in France, and was buried in Versailles when in 1937 she died at the age of 75.

———————————◆———————————

What type of text is *Ethan Frome*?

Society novel

The one thing that *Ethan Frome* is *not* is the 'society novel' for which Edith Wharton and Henry James (1843–1916) are most famous. If you have read or seen the film versions of Edith Wharton's *The Age of Innocence* (1920) or Henry James's *The Portrait of a Lady* (1881) or *The Wings of the Dove* (1902) you will be familiar with this kind of text. It dissects the manners and pretensions of the rich, the kind of people who were referred to as 'ladies' and 'gentlemen', and who spent their endless leisure time in the cultivation of taste and polite conversation. Their money was spent on large houses, servants, expensive clothes, and visits to Europe. The American rich were a privileged class of 'new money' people (sometimes known as 'nouveau riche') who sought to imitate the 'old money' lifestyle of the European aristocracy, but lacked the recognised family traditions.

Regional or 'local color' novel

The people in *Ethan Frome* are the opposite of the characters in a 'society novel' in every way. They are poor – so poor that they sit indoors in the cold with overcoats on because they cannot afford to heat their homes. They have no servants – they have to do everything for themselves. They fear the cost of illness. Their lives are bleak. They live in the mountain valleys, which become cut off in the snow. The city with its bustle and modernity is alien to them.

In these respects *Ethan Frome* could be described as a 'regional' or 'local color' novel. Such novels were popular in America at the turn of the twentieth century. They were usually written by women, they explored the lives of women in their own, regional settings – but as far as Edith Wharton was concerned, they did so through 'rose-coloured spectacles'. *Ethan Frome* announces itself as a story about a man, and is ruthlessly unsentimental in its representation of the lives of poor women and the cold society they inhabit.

Romance novel

There is one respect in which *Ethan Frome* does have something in common with a novel of old New York society, such as *The Age of Innocence*. In both 'backwoods' rural New England and 'sophisticated' urban New York there is the same taboo against divorce: if a marriage fails then the two partners must stay married because that is what society expects them to do.

This theme of a forbidden, adulterous lover is one that many nineteenth-century writers influenced by the Romantic movement had explored – most notably Charlotte Brontë in *Jane Eyre* (1847), Anne Brontë in *The Tenant of Wildfell Hall* (1848) and Nathaniel Hawthorne in *The Scarlet Letter* (1850).

Earlier novels had been known as 'romances' (the French word for novel is *roman*: the word originally referred to the Roman languages and did not carry the modern link with love). A Romance novel:

- is usually set in an earlier time;
- is more concerned with adventures than the thoughts and feelings of characters;
- concerns people in positions of power or privilege;
- frequently contains elements of magic or the supernatural.

Some of the elements of Romance were picked up by writers associated with the Romantic movement, with the difference that the Romantics became more concerned with ordinary people, and with feelings. As a literary genre influencing the novel, however, Romanticism eventually subsided in favour of Realism.

Realist novel

One novel which prepared the way for the harsh realism of *Ethan Frome* was *Madame Bovary* (1857), a study of adultery and suicide by the French writer Gustave Flaubert (1821–1880). Novels of Social Realism, such as those produced by Flaubert:

- have as their subject ordinary people, usually from the middle class;
- pay attention to the material detail of life, so that a writer may dwell on the description of a worn-out glove or the decoration of a room;
- examine the relationships between people, especially emotional relationships;
- often end on a note of defeat or disappointment.

Edith Wharton read novels by French writers in French, and her fellow writer and friend Henry James had met and been influenced by Flaubert.

Gothic writing

Gothic writing is a particular Romantic genre characterised by:

- remote or ancient settings;
- characters who exhibit extremes of behaviour, bordering on madness;
- a hint of dark secrets;
- an element of the supernatural.

Although the era of high Gothic had been a hundred years earlier, the success of Bram Stoker's *Dracula* (1897), published only fourteen years before *Ethan Frome*, reflected a revival of interest in the supernatural, while the late Victorian interest in ghosts carries over into *Tales of Men and Ghosts*, published by Edith Wharton in 1910, immediately before *Ethan Frome*.

✦ *Activity*

Apply the characteristics of each of the three genres listed above (Romance, Realism, Gothic writing) to *Ethan Frome*, and discuss whether the novel contains characteristics of one or more of these genres.

✦

How was *Ethan Frome* produced?

Origins

Edith Wharton made the following comments in her autobiography, *A Backward Glance* (1934):

> *Ethan Frome* shocked my readers less than
> *Summer*,° but it was frequently criticised as 'painful'
> and at first had much less success than my previous
> books. I have a clearer recollection of its beginnings
> than of those of my other tales, through the singular
> accident that its first pages were written – in French!
> I had determined, when we came to live in Paris, to
> polish and enlarge my French vocabulary; for
> though I had spoken the language since the age of
> four I had never had much occasion to talk it, for
> any length of time, with cultivated people, having
> usually, since my marriage, wandered through
> France as a tourist. ... To bring my idioms up to
> date I asked [a friend] to find, among his friends, a
> young professor who would come and talk with me
> two or three times a week. An amiable young man
> was found; but being too amiable ever to correct my
> spoken mistakes, he finally hit on the expedient of
> asking me to prepare an 'exercise' before each visit.
> The easiest thing for me to write was a story; and
> thus the French version of *Ethan Frome* was begun,
> and carried on for a few weeks. Then the lessons
> were given up, and the copy-book containing my
> 'exercise' vanished for ever. But a few years later,
> during one of our summer sojourns at The Mount,°
> a distant glimpse of Bear Mountain brought Ethan
> back to my memory, and the following winter in
> Paris I wrote the tale as it now stands, reading my
> morning's work aloud to Walter Berry [a relative

and close friend], who was as familiar as I was with the lives led in those half-deserted villages before the coming of motor and telephone. We talked the tale over page by page, so that its accuracy and 'atmosphere' is doubly assured – and I mention this because not long since, in an article by an American literary critic, I saw *Ethan Frome* cited as an interesting example of a successful New England story written by some one who knew nothing of New England! *Ethan Frome* was written after I had spent ten years in the hill-region where the scene is laid, during which years I had come to know well the aspect, dialect and mental and moral attitude of the hill-people.

(Wharton, 1934 (1972 edition, p. 295))

This comment was written twenty or so years after the publication of the novel. Edith Wharton's autobiography takes its title from Walt Whitman's (1819–1892) phrase 'A backward glance o'er travelled roads'. This and following comments show Edith Wharton looking back on what it had meant to be a writer when she engaged in the production of *Ethan Frome*.

Control of writing

Edith Wharton confessed to having a long apprenticeship as a writer. She spent a long time finding out how to write in a way that satisfied her:

I went on steadily trying to 'find out how to'; but I wrote two or three novels without feeling that I had made much progress. It was not until I wrote 'Ethan Frome' that I suddenly felt the artisan's full control of his implements. When 'Ethan Frome' first appeared I was severely criticised by the reviewers for what was considered the clumsy structure of the tale. I had pondered long on this structure, had felt its peculiar difficulties, and possible awkwardness, but could think of no alternative which would serve as well in the given case; and though I am far from thinking 'Ethan Frome' my best novel, and am bored and even exasperated when I am told that it is, I am still sure that its structure is not its weak point.

(Wharton, 1934 (1972, p. 209))

Aims of her writing

Edith Wharton also had a clear idea of the way that a story should be told – in such a way that the writer, if not the reader, knows that events are moving towards an inevitable end:

It is always a necessity to me that the note of inevitableness should be sounded at the very opening of my tale, and that my characters should go forward to their ineluctable doom like 'murdered man' in 'The Pot of Basil'.° From the very first I know exactly what is going to happen to every one of them; their fate is settled beyond rescue, and I have but to watch and record.

(Wharton, 1934 (1972, p. 204))

Of *Ethan Frome* in particular, she wrote:

But the book to the making of which I brought the greatest joy and the fullest ease was 'Ethan Frome'. For years I had wanted to draw life as it really was in the derelict mountain villages of New England, a life even in my time, and a thousandfold a generation earlier, utterly unlike that seen through the rose-coloured spectacles of my predecessors,

Mary Wilkins and Sarah Orne Jewett.* In those days the snow-bound villages of Western Massachusetts were still grim places, morally and physically: insanity, incest and slow mental and moral starvation were hidden away behind the paintless wooden house-fronts of the long village street, or in the isolated farm-houses on the neighbouring hills; and Emily Brontë would have found as savage tragedies in our remote valleys as on her Yorkshire moors.

(Wharton, 1934 (1972, p. 294))

The opening quotation in this section drew attention to the way that what Edith Wharton calls her 'tale' started life as an exercise for practising her French. Later she wrote it in English. She gives us a glimpse of how she felt about it in a letter written on 4 January 1911, when she was staying in the rue de Varenne in Paris:

I am driving harder and harder at that ridiculous nouvelle, which has grown into a large long-legged hobbledehoy of a young novel. 20,000 long it is already, and growing. I have to let its frocks down every day, and soon it will be in trousers! However, I see an end, for I'm over the hard explanatory part, and the *vitesse acquise* is beginning to rush me along. The scene is laid at Starkfield Mass, and the nearest cosmopolis is called Shadd's Falls. It amuses me to do that decor in the rue de Varenne.

(Lewis and Lewis, *The Letters of Edith Wharton*, 1988, p. 232)

The process of composition

If you ever imagine that writers produce their books in one go then Edith Wharton is the person to show you otherwise. She wrote her novels with a pen on the thin kind of writing paper that we now use for air mail letters. She made changes as she wrote, and actually took a pair of scissors to her draft pages, cutting out paragraphs that she liked and pasting them on to another sheet of paper. Other changes – to words or phrases – would be made, and then the whole thing would be typed up (Edith Wharton was wealthy enough to employ a secretary). Further changes would be made to the typed manuscript before it was ready to be sent off. If you turn to the Appendix on page 169 you will see an example of the cutting and pasting method used by Edith Wharton.

Edith Wharton later confided to her diary what writing a novel was like:

> The beginning: a ride through a Spring wood
> The middle: the Gobi desert
> The end: going down the Cresta run⬦
>
> (Diary, 10 December 1934)

The last comment seems particularly relevant when you discover how this novel ends.

Ethan Frome as commercial product

A story only enters the public arena when it becomes printed and published, and for that to happen certain things must be in place. There must be a market for stories, a readership which is willing to buy them. The story is part of commercial activity.

The end of the nineteenth and the beginning of the twentieth century was the era of American popular magazines such as *Scribner's Magazine*. Immediately prior to the publication of *Ethan Frome* Edith Wharton had published a number of short stories in *Scribner's Magazine* and *Century*. These stories were published as *Tales of Men and Ghosts* in 1910 and revealed an interest in the subconscious, ghosts and the supernatural. They reflect a dark, turbulent period in Edith Wharton's life. *Ethan Frome* made its first appearance in instalments in *Scribner's Magazine* from August 1911 to November 1911. It appeared in book form in September, and initially the sales were disappointing. By November 4,200 had been sold, and in a letter to Charles Scribner dated 11 November, Edith Wharton expressed surprise that it had not sold more. Sales had reached nearly 7,000 by February 1912, but it would not become a commercial success until another thirty years had passed.

✦ *Activity*

To complete the circle, the story which had started life as an untitled French exercise was translated back into French with the title *Hiver* ('Winter'). What is the significance of this title?

✦

How does *Ethan Frome* present its subject?

Time and sequencing

Edith Wharton's introduction to *Ethan Frome* concentrates on its structure – on how the story is told. This principally involves the use of time as a narrative device, a point reinforced by her insistence to her publishers that the dots on pages 32 and 123 be emphasised to suggest the passing of time. *They are unusual, and if you are keeping a reading log you might make a note of this.* The reader is also taken backwards and forwards in time – events are not narrated in the sequence in which they actually occurred.

✦ *Activity*

On the first page of the story the reader is told that the narrator first saw Ethan Frome 'several years ago': a description of Ethan then follows. So, right from the beginning the reader is taken back in time from the 'now' of the story being told, to the visit to Starkfield some years previously. The sequence of events from the start of the story up to the end of Chapter 2 goes something like this:

1 Present narrative moment (the moment of the story being spoken or written);
2 Some years ago in Starkfield;
3 Story moves forward to the snowstorm, and the dots … ;
4 Story goes back twenty four years to the dance;
5 Story goes even further back, to the year before, when Mattie first arrived in Starkfield, and Ethan found himself getting on well with her;
6 Forward to the period before the dance, when Zeena was complaining about Mattie, suggesting that she might move on;
7 Forward to the dance and the journey back to the farm.

This is the narrative sequence. Now draw a diagram like the one on page 144, and plot these events in the order in which they occurred chronologically (in time), to see the difference between the narrative and the chronological sequence. The seven boxes along the line represent the seven 'events' listed above, and 'number 1' is already in place. It is the 'now' at the beginning of the book, the present narrative moment, and it is followed by *earlier* events:

Chronological sequence and narrative sequence						
Earliest event						Latest event
The dance (24 years before the snowstorm) ↓				The snowstorm (some years ago) ↓		
						1
The 'now': the moment when ↑ the story is being told						

Now go to Chapter 3 (for a relatively straightforward example) or to Chapter 9 and read to the end (for something more complicated and time-consuming!) and in pairs or fours work out both the narrative and the chronological sequence, as above. Display these on a large sheet of paper and present a short report to the rest of the class.

Point of view and focalisation in Ethan Frome

Although the narrator doesn't hear the story from Ethan, he begins to tell it through Ethan's eyes. In Chapters 1–9, events are perceived from Ethan's point of view. This shapes the way the reader sees the other characters in the story. Other characters speak and have a point of view. Consider what happens when the point of view is shifted – when what is called the 'focalisation' is changed.

◆ *Activities*

1 Re-read pages 60–62, which tells how Zeena comes to Starkfield to look after Ethan's mother and ends up marrying him. Rewrite the passage from Zeena's point of view. In a small group, read each other's versions. What light is thrown on Ethan's character when he is seen through Zeena's eyes? How do the new versions change the position of the reader?

2 Discuss the following statements and questions about Ethan, using evidence from the text:
   - Ethan has an 'awful mean time' (p. 105) and his relationship with Mattie is understandable. He longs for companionship. His 'bitter querulous' wife has blighted his chance of happiness (p. 98).
   - Ethan is full of self pity. He is a weak man who marries for the wrong reasons.
   - Ethan is an honourable man who fulfils his responsibilities to his parents and to his wife.
   - Ethan deserves what he gets.
   - Ethan is self-centred. He is intent on gratifying his sexual desires after the relationship with his wife breaks down.

   Do you think that your response is the one that the text seems to be encouraging, or do you think you are resisting the way the text would like you to respond?

3 Discuss the following questions about the narrative point of view:
   a As the story unfolds, do you always remember, or soon start to forget, that you are seeing events through the eyes of the outsider who has come to do a job at the power-house?

   Do you remember or forget that this account is drawing on the details that have been given to this visitor by Mrs Ned Hale and Harmon Gow?
   b What do you know about this narrator? What are the advantages and disadvantages of having him as a

storyteller? Draw two columns and see if it is easier to identify the advantages or the disadvantages.

c Whereabouts in the text is it signalled that the narrator is getting details of the story from someone else? Does Edith Wharton make any attempt to remind you of this fact?

Showing and telling

Edith Wharton believed very strongly that fiction should teach the reader something, but by 'showing' rather than 'telling'. She was a close friend of the novelist Henry James (1843–1916), who disapproved of narratives in which the writer suddenly interrupts the story and tells the reader what to think about it. There is an example of the kind of thing Henry James and Edith Wharton disapproved of at the end of the second chapter of *Hard Times* by Charles Dickens (1812–1870). Dickens has shown the reader a schoolroom from the nineteenth century in which the children are identified by numbers ('Girl number twenty') and not by their names, and in which facts and nothing but facts are to form the curriculum. It is exactly the kind of teaching method recommended in an official manual of the times. The narrator then tells the reader that the teacher is called Mr M'Choakumchild and that he intends to make the children recite by heart points of the compass and the rivers and mountains of the world. In case you have missed the point, the narrator goes on to tell the reader:

> Ah, rather overdone, M'Choakumchild. If he had only learnt a little less, how infinitely better he might have taught much more!
> (Charles Dickens, *Hard Times*, 1854)

When you read *Hard Times* you would probably agree with this, but to Edith Wharton it is better if the writer stops short of telling the reader what to think. Edith Wharton approved of Dickens's desire to influence his readers, but not of this blunt method, involving satirical names and authorial intervention. In her unpublished article 'Fiction and Criticism' she illustrated the way that the novel should teach without preaching by quoting Guy de Maupassant's (1850–1893) remark: 'if a book teaches a lesson it must be in spite of its author, *by the mere force of the facts he narrates*'.◇

✦ *Activity*

What kinds of stories teach lessons without containing characters or narrators who preach sermons? Edith Wharton had in mind the novels she admired written by French novelists and by Henry James. Shorter examples are needed here, and the simplest are those kinds of stories that pass from generation to generation as fables, folk tales / fairy stories, parables and allegories. Here they are in outline – it would be better to read the full versions:

> **An Aesop fable – 'The Tortoise and the Hare'**
> A tortoise and a hare agree to have a race. The hare
> is so far ahead in the race that he decides to have a
> rest. He falls asleep under a tree and the tortoise
> who has kept going without stopping passes him
> and crosses the finishing line first.

In pairs, discuss the moral argument of this story. Can you resist this argument, and through a resistant◇ reading identify other agendas in this text?

> **A folk tale/fairy story – 'Little Red Riding Hood'**
> Little Red Riding Hood is warned not to stray from
> the path when she takes some food to her
> grandmother. On the way she meets a wolf in the
> forest. The wolf recommends a short-cut to her

grandmother's house, and when she arrives the wolf
has reached her grandmother's house before her,
eaten her grandmother, and is about to eat Little
Red Riding Hood when the Woodman comes to her
rescue and kills the wolf with his axe.

In pairs discuss the moral argument of this story. Can you
resist this argument, and through a resistant reading identify
other agendas in this text?

Note all your responses in your reading log. You will need
to draw on them again in an activity in the section 'Who reads
Ethan Frome?' on page 153, which asks you to think about
what the novel is meant to teach the reader about Ethan Frome
and his situation. You may wish to go to this section (with its
resistant reading activity on page 155) now.

Opposites

Literary works are often structured in terms of oppositions
such as 'good/evil', 'hero/villain', 'reason/emotion'. It is often
thought that people make sense of the world through such
opposing concepts. Sometimes these oppositions are seen in a
positive and negative light with, for example, 'reason' being
the superior concept and 'emotion' inferior.

✦ *Activity*

a   Consider *Ethan Frome* in terms of the oppositions which
    are at work and see how they shape meaning and how that
    meaning shifts as the oppositions shift. Choose one set of
    opposites and discuss how it applies to each of the main
    characters in the novel (Mattie, then Zeena, and finally
    Ethan):
    • Negation – Affirmation
    • Vitality – Deadness/sickness
    • Spring – Winter
    • Hopes and dreams – Reality

b Sometimes the oppositions can be grouped so that they form a triangle. Consider each of the characters in the triangle in relation to each other, and use the triangle as a frame on which to make notes about the way one character is affected by the  presence of another. Consider what difference it would make to the diagram if you put either Zeena or Mattie at the top. Should one or other of these be placed there, rather than Ethan?

Characterisation

The reader builds up a picture of characters through what the text shows them to say, through what it shows them doing, and through what others, including the narrator, say about them.

✦ *Activity*

Imagine that the narrator returns to Starkfield ten years later to discover that either Mattie, Ethan or Zeena has just died. Working in small groups, gather the evidence provided by the sources suggested above (what the character says in the story, what the character does or has done, and what others say about him or her), and build up a picture of your chosen character. Shape the material you have gathered into the following three texts:

- an appreciation given by the minister in a church service;
- a report in the local paper the *Bettsbridge Eagle*;
- a monologue from Jotham Powell, who used to work for Ethan.

In a commentary, show how you have tried to make these three reports differ from one another.

Setting

The setting, particularly the landscape and weather, plays an important part in the story. It is more than background – it is a presence. The director of the film version (*Ethan Frome*, directed by John Madden, 1992) has emphasised how much the setting contributed to the atmosphere.

✦ *Activity*

In the role of a film-maker preparing to meet the art and lighting directors, draw up the following chart and make notes about three or four scenes so that you can discuss how best to represent the setting and create the mood.

Scene	Setting	Mood	Colour/tone

Language and rhetoric
Irony, imagery and grammar

Irony occurs in language when the writing says one thing and means another. It is quite possible that the following description of Ethan is ironic:

> Having satisfied himself that there was no risk of immediate discovery he went back to the kitchen with a lighter step, and found Mattie disconsolately removing the last scraps of pickle from the floor.
>
> 'It's all right, Matt. Come back and finish supper,' he commanded her.
>
> Completely reassured, she shone on him through tear-hung lashes, and his soul swelled with pride as he saw how his tone subdued her. She did not even

ask what he had done. Except when he was steering
a big log down the mountain to his mill he had
never known such a thrilling sense of mastery.

(p. 70)

It may not sound ironic, but it is the situation and the context
that often gives the reader the clue. Here, all that has happened
is that Ethan has re-assembled a broken pickle dish and told
Mattie not to worry about it any more. His confidence and
mastery prove ill-founded even in this, because Zeena
discovers the breakage soon after her return, and this leads
directly to the expulsion of Mattie.

Look for other examples of irony on pages 94 (when the
broken pickle dish is discovered) and 55 (the treatment of
Mattie by her relatives).

Imagery usually refers to figurative language – metaphors,
similes, pathetic fallacy. What does 'winter' stand for? Take,
for example, any one chapter and look for references to the
cold, the winter and the harsh conditions. What is the effect of
these images? There are glimpses of a warmer world: look at
pages 26, 49, 71, 112 and 120 and comment on these in your
reading log.

Grammar is a description of how language is ordered and
organised. This organisation can be considered at text,
sentence or word level.

Imagery and irony show the effects of language at text level,
but you can break down these effects by looking at the
structural parts – the nouns, verbs, adjectives and adverbs, the
sentence, phrases and paragraphs that contribute to these
effects.

✦ *Activity*

a In pairs, take one of the four pages referred to in the
sections on 'irony' and 'imagery' above, and with the aid of
a photocopy, use a set of colours to highlight:

- sentence length;
- paragraph length;
- clauses and phrases within sentences;
- the number of nouns;
- the number of verbs;
- the number of adjectives;
- the number of adverbs;
- the number of words with three or more syllables.

In pairs, discuss the effect created by some or all of the features you have identified.

b Compare your findings with three other pairs who have taken the three other pages. Are different scenes characterised by a different emphasis within the grammar?

Ideology

Ideology is the set of the beliefs that the story either endorses or challenges. You can approach this by considering a series of questions about the central tragedy of the three characters. In pairs begin to think about the community's belief systems and the way that this might contrast with the reader's beliefs and the beliefs of the narrator.

✦ *Activity*

a How does the Starkfield community view this tragedy? What do they think caused it, and how should it be judged?

b How does the story intend the reader to view this tragedy? What is the story encouraging the reader to identify as the cause of the tragedy, and how does it seem to want us to judge it?

c Is it possible to resist the reading that the story seems to want you, as a reader, to make?

You may be helped towards an answer to the last question by considering how others have read this story.

———————————— ✦ ————————————

Who reads *Ethan Frome*? How do they interpret it?

It is useful to regard a first reading of a novel as a provisional reading. It is likely to change as you encounter other people's readings, some of which may cause you to revise your original response, while others may reinforce it.

Contemporary readings

The reviews that appeared when the book was first published were generally favourable. This is from *The Bookman*, January 1912:

> Mrs Wharton has more than satisfied one's expectation, and her art has never been shown to greater advantage than in this story of Ethan Frome, the young Massachusetts farmer. It is a tragedy, almost unendurably poignant, but justified by its inevitableness. From his youth Fate dealt hardly with Ethan. His father died, leaving him a bleak unproductive farm, and a failing saw-mill. ... Poverty makes Ethan helpless; money might have saved two lives, if not three, but there is none. So the blow falls in the last act that is to consign the three to a living death. It is a beautiful, sad, but intensely human story, working out to its final conclusion with all the inevitability of a great Greek tragedy.

An American reviewer, in the New York *Call* (4 February 1912) makes a similar observation about the effect of poverty, arguing that we should see Ethan, Mattie and Zeena as 'wrecked mariners' whose story supports an argument for socialism: if a crew of wrecked sailors are washed up on a desert island, we don't expect them to endure their fate without help.

A feminist reading

Ethan Frome, like Nathaniel Hawthorne's *The Scarlet Letter*, can be read as an exposure of the flaws in long-established patriarchal (male dominated) cultures. Although in both novels it is the women who seem to exercise power, they do so within a set of rules established by the Puritan men. Both novels provide an examination of masculinity (the central male in each case is weak) and ultimately they show the way that society insisted – and in many contexts still insists – that unless men and women behave in certain, contrasting, conventional ways they will be open to criticism.

John Madden, the director of the film version of *Ethan Frome*, said that he regarded Ethan as 'potentially wimpish' because he did not have the courage to run away with Mattie. He says this to justify some of the changes that he made in the film. In response, the critic Janet Beer Goodwyn (BBC Education, 1995) has said that the wimpish thing would have been to run off and give in to his selfish feelings – that he is courageous to give priority to his conscience.

But Edith Wharton did not identify with the feminist movement, or the 'New Women' – women who were more educated and independent than their predecessors, and who were beginning to question traditional female roles at the end of the nineteenth century. The influence of her parents and her background remained powerful in the way she lived and the views she expressed publicly: it is in her fiction that the reader sees a more developed analysis of that society. It was in fiction that women could ask questions of a kind that would have been unacceptable in their public, everyday speech and letters. This contrast should not be surprising: from all we know William Shakespeare (1564–1616) and Jane Austen (1775–1817) lived very unremarkable, ordered lives and seemed to believe in order. That did not stop them from questioning in their writings the way that things were ordered.

A resistant reading

It is certainly true that in her outer life Wharton accepted and conformed to the rules that her society demanded. In the years after the First World War (1914–1918), when she saw the old order increasingly being questioned she came increasingly to value an ordered, rule-governed society. Nevertheless, in her pre-war fiction she makes the reader aware of the inhibiting effects of those rules. This is evident in *Ethan Frome*:

> He knew that most young men made nothing at all
> of giving a pretty girl a kiss, and he remembered
> that the night before, when he had put his arm
> about Mattie, she had not resisted. But that had
> been out-of-doors, under the open irresponsible
> night. Now, in the warm lamplit room, with all its
> ancient implications of conformity and order, she
> seemed infinitely farther away from him and more
> unapproachable.
>
> (pp.73–74)

This is similar to the argument made by Thomas Hardy in *Tess of the d'Urbervilles* (1891) and by Nathaniel Hawthorne in *The Scarlet Letter* (1850), that social rules are made by humans, and that nature does not judge humans in the harsh way that society does.

✦ *Activity*

Review *Ethan Frome* as a whole, in the light of these comments and the notes you were invited to make in an activity in an earlier section 'Showing and telling' (pp. 146–148). Then discuss your response to these two questions:

- What is the moral argument of this story?
- Can you as a reader resist this argument, and through a resistant reading identify other agendas in this text?

A psycho-analytic reading

One feature of psycho-analysis is that it emphasises the way that, in dreams, events that really concern you appear symbolically – if you are anxious about being bullied you might dream of being chased by packs of wolves. The sleigh ride has been read symbolically – as a symbolic sexual experience. Mattie and Ethan are clinging together, they thrill to the point of ecstasy, the language suggests the passion they have not been able to enjoy in life.

There are other ways of reading *Ethan Frome* psycho-analytically. The critic Shari Benstock draws on such readings in this extract from her biography of Edith Wharton:

> This little tale – a 'volumelet' less than a hundred
> pages in print – bitterly condemns the human
> weakness and inertia that chain people in what
> Edith once called 'sterile pain'. ... Emotionally and
> materially *Ethan Frome* is a rigid moonscape. While
> the imaginary Starkfield has no intellectual
> equivalent to Lenox life, it is not without communal
> activities – sleigh rides, church socials and dances,
> like the one from which a flushed and smiling
> Mattie emerges when we first see her. The isolation
> of the Frome household that destroys its inhabitants
> and renders Mattie a younger version of Zeena is
> self-enforced by separation from the human
> community and a turning inward on themselves.
>
> (Shari Benstock, *No Gifts from Chance: a
> Biography of Edith Wharton*, 1994, p. 248)

A post-colonial reading

The 'original' story told of America, the one that rather overlooked the culture and history of Native Americans, is the story that is celebrated on Thanksgiving Day, when the successful beginnings of the Pilgrim 'Fathers' colony is commemorated. It is also the beginning of the myth of the American Dream. A post-colonial reading of Ethan Frome would draw attention to the novel's questioning of the American Dream (Ethan's dream of escape finishes up as a situation of nightmare) and of other New England stories, such as the one that says that American literature begins with white Anglo-Saxon male writers such as Ralph Waldo Emerson (1803–1882) and Henry David Thoreau (1817–1862).

Black book version

Another way of approaching *Ethan Frome* is to consider the various versions of it and to look at the idea of 'difference'. There is the eight-page French version, the exercise that Edith Wharton produced in a black book (the one she thought had vanished, but now in the keeping of Yale University) for her French teacher in Paris. This had three characters: Hart, his wife Anna and his cousin Mattie. The difference between this early version and *Ethan Frome* – apart from the change of names – is that you learn quite early on that Hart and Mattie have admitted their love for one another. The French version also allows the possibility that they go beyond the brother/sister relationship to which they have sworn to stick. Hart's wife goes away to visit a specialist doctor in Worcester; Hart and Mattie are alone in the house together. But he is resolved not take advantage of her (as he sees it) and roughly tells her to go to bed as he has work to do. What happens next is unclear, and there are other textual clues, such as the fact that Hart's wife does not come back the next day but the day after the next, that allow for the possibility that the two characters become lovers, as they do in the film version.

Film version

You may have the opportunity to see the film version with Liam Neeson and Patricia Arquette (1992). In this version it is clearly shown that Ethan and Mattie have a sexual relationship, and there is a warmth and passion kept in check in the version that Edith Wharton came to write in 1911. This raises the question of why the published version of the story was written in the way that it was, with a clear indication that though they may have kissed, there was no sexual relationship between Ethan and Mattie.

It is possible that this is so because Edith Wharton knew it to be unacceptable to the society to which she belonged. Both Thomas Hardy (1840–1928) and Kate Chopin (1850–1904) had been condemned when they published novels that presented adulterous sexual relationships in a sympathetic light. Hardy stopped writing novels after the furore over *Jude the Obscure* (1895). For Kate Chopin, a woman writer from within the society that disapproved of her novel *The Awakening* (1899), in which a married woman takes a lover, the condemnation was devastating. Chopin never completed another novel, was ignored by people she had formerly considered friends, and died not very long after the publication of the damning reviews.

This explanation is the reason given for the change by the film screen-writer of *Ethan Frome*, Richard Nelson. Interviewed for the BBC (BBC 1995) he said that because we know that Edith Wharton had a brief, passionate affair with the journalist Morton Fullerton at about the time she was writing the novel, and because we know from her private writing that she could write with passion and frankness about sexual relationships, he felt justified in changing the story to show that Ethan and Mattie seized two brief opportunities to make love. It is an element which he believes Edith Wharton would have introduced if she were alive today, writing for a modern audience.

✦ *Activity*

Imagine that you are a member of a team that is preparing a version of *Ethan Frome* for television. Divide into groups of six or eight. Half the group should prepare an argument that the film you are making should not include a scene which suggests a sexual relationship between Ethan and Mattie, and the other half should argue the opposite. Then meet as a full group, elect a chair, and discuss the issue in a full screenplay meeting. You may need to consider:

• the kind of television film you are making;
• the audience and their possible knowledge of the book;
• what the book has to say about this relationship;
• how a change to the story would mean a change to the characterisation;
• the impact of the ending if we know that Mattie and Ethan were once lovers.

If you have time, your group may wish to go on to discuss the pros and cons of making other changes that were made in the film version, and whether you wish to incorporate them into your television version. These were:

• the change of narrator from a visiting engineer to a new minister;
• the change whereby Zeena is presented as a warmer, more attractive young woman;
• the emphasis on the visual beauty, rather than the harshness of the winter landscape.

Reading *Ethan Frome* as metafiction

In *A Feast of Words* (1977) the critic Cynthia Griffin Wolff says that the subject of *Ethan Frome* is its structure – the way that the story is told – and argues that there are strong reasons why it should be read primarily as a story about storytelling. So what is the relationship between structure and 'meta-fiction'? 'Metafiction' is fiction which draws attention to the fact that it is fiction, that it is the outcome of the act of writing.

An example of this technique is *If on a Winter's Night a Traveller* (1979) by Italo Calvino, which begins:

> You are about to begin reading Italo Calvino's new
> novel, *If on a winter's night a traveller*. Relax.
> Concentrate. Dispel every other thought. Let the
> world around you fade. Best to close the door; the
> TV is always on in the next room. Tell the others
> right away, 'No, I don't want to watch the TV!'
> Raise your voice – they won't hear you otherwise.
> ... Find the most comfortable position: seated,
> stretched out, curled up, or lying flat. Flat on your
> back, on your side, on your stomach. In an easy
> chair, on the sofa, in the rocker, the deck chair, on
> the hassock. On the hammock, if you have a
> hammock. On top of your bed, of course, or in the
> bed. ... having your feet up is the first condition for
> enjoying a read.

So here the writer draws our attention to the act of reading, while in other novels, such as *Tristram Shandy* (1759–1767) by Laurence Sterne (1713–1768), attention is drawn to the act of writing by having blank pages for the reader to insert their own character descriptions, and chapter numbers that don't follow one another.

Cynthia Wolff does not argue that Edith Wharton is trying to do any of these light, humorous things. Instead she emphasises the way that Ethan, Mattie and to a lesser extent the narrator, are characters who like to dream. Ethan in particular lives in a world in which the imaginary is far more inviting than the reality. He marries Zeena because he dreams of what it would be like to have company and not to be alone. The reality turns out to be terrible. So he dreams of what it would be like to live with Mattie. Similarly the narrator – and this is Wolff's central point – puts together a story about these people which draws on what he has been told but is an interpretation of the basic facts he learns and of the encounters with the three people, who are now in old age. Note in your reading log where the use of three dots at the end of a paragraph contributes to this jigsaw effect.

✦ *Activities*

1 Devise the outline for a short story, and then begin the story. As you write it, draw attention to the fact that you are writing it, by referring to the circumstances around you – the pen or computer you are using, the room you are in, the noises you can hear, the thoughts that come into your head, a feeling of hunger or cold, these kinds of things.

2 Applying different readings to *Ethan Frome*

a Working in a group of four or five, each person should select one of the following approaches:
   - a feminist reading;
   - a resistant reading;
   - a psycho-analytic reading;
   - a comparative reading (drawing on film and book);
   - a metafictional reading;
   - a post-colonial reading.

   Building on the work you have done already, prepare a presentation to be made to the other members of the group.

b When the class next meets, form into new groups made up of people taking the same approach, that is a feminist group, a resistant reading group, and so on. Try out your presentation on this group, all of whom will be 'experts' in your chosen area, and obtain some feedback from them.

   Having made any necessary adjustments to your paper, return to your original group and offer your presentation to them.

c If there is time, decide which of the presentations your group has heard has been most successful. This should then be presented to the whole class. Questions may be taken at the end of each presentation. When all the presentations have been made, reflect in your reading log on what it is that makes a presentation successful.

d Finally, expand your own paper into an essay or extended piece of writing. You should by now have a considerable bank of material on which to draw. Make sure that you allow for changes of direction. You may be inspired to switch to a different type of reading from the one you originally chose, especially if you have heard other readings that were particularly stimulating!

GLOSSARY

From Edith Wharton's Introduction

15   'La Grande Bretêche': a story by the French writer
Honoré de Balzac (1799–1850), told by several narrators
'The Ring and the Book': a long poem by Robert
Browning (1812–1889), showing a single murder seen
from a number of different points of view

From *Ethan Frome*

19   bay: a reddish-brown horse
pre-trolley: before the arrival of the electric tram car – a
bus that runs on rails

22   power-house: a building containing machines for
generating electricity, a recent invention in the time when
the story is set

23   Carcel lamp: an oil lamp with a clockwork device to
pump the oil to the wick, invented in 1798 by the
Frenchman B. G. Carcel (1750–1812)

33   Dipper ... Orion: constellations of stars. The Big Dipper is
part of the constellation of the Great Bear, and Orion is
named after Orion the Hunter from Greek mythology. In
the text it indicates something big, predatory and cold –
but also beautiful.

35   fascinator: a lace scarf worn over the head by women.
Notice the colour. How does this colour contrast
symbolically with the whiteness of the surrounding snow?
Virginia reel: a kind of country dance in which the
partners are face to face or in opposite lines

37   Aldebaran ... the Pleiades: the first is a double star, the
second another constellation, representing in Greek
mythology the seven daughters of Atlas. According to
myth they had been pursued by Orion. The contrast in
scale with the watchers is worth noting.

40   turnip-watch: a thick silver watch

44   cutter: a small, light sleigh
roan colt: a chestnut, red or brown young horse, with
grey or white interspersed in the colour of its coat

48   **hemlock belt:** a stretch of trees, containing hemlock
     spruces
50   **counterpane:** a cover for a bed
     crimping-pins: pins used to make the hair wavy
54   **Curfew ...:** from a ballad 'Curfew must not ring tonight'
     (1867) by Rose Hartwick Thorpe (1850–1939)
     'The Lost Chord': a popular sentimental song, with words
     by Adelaide Anne Procter (1825–1864) and music by Sir
     Arthur Sullivan (1842–1900)
     pot-pourri from 'Carmen': a collection of musical pieces
     from the opera *Carmen* (1875) by the French composer
     Georges Bizet (1838–1875). It may be significant that the
     story deals with passion, violence and death among
     Spanish gypsies, in contrast to the suppressed emotions of
     the New Englanders.
     stenography: the art of writing in shorthand
57   **sorrel:** a yellowish or reddish brown – here referring to
     the horse
78   **traveller's joy:** a vine that flowers spectacularly in summer
     – some irony here!
103 **huckabuck towel:** a towel made of a rough, coarse linen
     match-safe: a matchbox

From the Resource Notes

137 *Summer:* a novella by Edith Wharton also set in New
     England and first published in 1917. Warmer and more
     passionate than *Ethan Frome* (called a 'hot *Ethan*' by
     Edith Wharton), it tells the story of a secret illicit affair in
     an eastern Massachusetts village during one summer.
     The Mount: the name of the large country house in
     Lenox, western Massachusetts, from where Edith
     Wharton explored the region that is the setting for both
     Ethan Frome and *Summer*
139 **'The Pot of Basil':** This is a reference to the poem
     'Isabella: or, The Pot of Basil', published in *Lamia ... and
     other poems* in 1820 by John Keats (1795–1821). The
     poem tells the story (taken from *The Decameron*, a
     collection of stories published between1349 and 1351 by

the Italian writer Giovanni Boccaccio (1313–1375)) of the murder of Lorenzo, a poor clerk, by the two brothers of Isabella. Isabella, the only daughter of a merchant family, had fallen in love with the clerk, but the brothers were determined that she should marry someone wealthy: Lorenzo is thus doomed, and described as the 'murdered man' as he is tricked into going for a ride in the forest with the brothers. Isabella later discovers Lorenzo's body and at the end of the poem is shown pining over a pot containing a basil plant, in which, rather macabrely, she has placed her dead lover's head.

140 **Mary Wilkins and Sarah Orne Jewett:** Mary Eleanor Wilkins Freeman (1852–1930) and Sarah Orne Jewett (1849–1909), New England 'local color' writers, see page 133.

141 **Cresta run:** a long, twisting ice course for toboggans, built in 1884 on the side of a mountain at St Moritz, Switzerland

147 **'if a book teaches …':** Edith Wharton considered this an 'excellent definition of a good novel'. 'Fiction and Criticism' is an unpublished article in the Edith Wharton Collection in the Beinecke Library at Yale University, and the quotation is discussed by the critic Penelope Vita-Finzi in her book *Edith Wharton and the Art of Fiction* (1990).

resistant (reading): This is the process by which a reader resists the general argument of a story, and ask questions about the assumptions made in the story. A simple example: in many old monster films, the heroine will slip and fall while being pursued by the monster. This is meant to show her weakness, and usually requires someone to come to her rescue. In a resistant reading, the reader would ask why it is assumed that the woman will fall over and not the man who is accompanying her.

FURTHER READING

Books by Edith Wharton

The House of Mirth (1905)

Tales of Men and Ghosts (1910)

The Custom of the Country (1913)

'The Bunner Sisters' in *Xingu and Other Stories* (1916)

Summer (1917)

The Age of Innocence (1920) (available in a version edited by Janet Beer Goodwyn in the Cambridge Literature series (Cambridge University Press, 1995))

A Backward Glance (1934: autobiography)

The Buccaneers (1938)

Additional reading

Shari Benstock, *No Gifts from Chance: a Biography of Edith Wharton* (Hamish Hamilton, 1994)

Eleanor Dwight, *Edith Wharton: An Extraordinary Life* (Harry N. Abrams, 1994)

Gloria C. Erlich, *The Sexual Education of Edith Wharton* (University of California Press, 1992)

R. W. B. Lewis, *Edith Wharton* (Constable, 1975)

R. W. B. Lewis, *Edith Wharton: A Biography* (Vintage 1993; first published 1975)

R. W. B and N. Lewis (eds), *The Letters of Edith Wharton* (Simon & Schuster, 1988)

P. Vita-Finzi, *Edith Wharton and the Art of Fiction*, (Pinter, 1990)

Candace Waid, 'Introduction' in Edith Wharton, *A Backward Glance* (Everyman, 1993)

Carol Wershovan, *The Female Intruder in the Novels of Edith Wharton* (Fairleigh Dickinson Press, 1982)

Cynthia Griffin Wolff, *A Feast of Words: The Triumph of Edith Wharton* (Oxford University Press, 1977)

Film versions of books by Edith Wharton

Ethan Frome, with Liam Neeson and Patricia Arquette, directed by John Madden (1992) (obtainable on video by writing directly to American distributors Buena Vista Home Video Dept., CS Burbank, California 91521, USA)

The Age of Innocence directed by Martin Scorsese (1993)

The Buccaneers, executive producer Philippa Giles, BBC (1995)

Other resources

Edith Wharton and her Novels, BBC Education (1995) (This pack concentrates on the three novels that have been filmed, and includes a videotape, audiotape and set of notes. The interviews with the director and screenwriter of the film version of *Ethan Frome*, quoted above, are taken from the video.)

APPENDIX

Edith Wharton's writing method: the first page of the novel (see page 141)

CAMBRIDGE LITERATURE

Ben Jonson *The Alchemist*

William Wycherley *The Country Wife*

Robert Burns *Selected Poems*

William Blake *Selected Works*

Jane Austen *Pride and Prejudice*

Jane Austen *Emma*

Mary Shelley *Frankenstein*

Three Victorian Poets

Charlotte Brontë *Jane Eyre*

Emily Brontë *Wuthering Heights*

Nathaniel Hawthorne *The Scarlet Letter*

Charles Dickens *Hard Times*

Charles Dickens *Great Expectations*

George Eliot *Silas Marner*

Thomas Hardy *Far from the Madding Crowd*

Henrik Ibsen *A Doll's House*

Robert Louis Stevenson *Treasure Island*

Mark Twain *Huckleberry Finn*

Thomas Hardy *Tess of the d'Urbervilles*

Oscar Wilde   *The Importance of Being Earnest*

Kate Chopin   *The Awakening and other stories*

Anton Chekhov   *The Cherry Orchard*

James Joyce   *Dubliners*

Six Poets of the Great War

D. H. Lawrence   *Selected Short Stories*

Edith Wharton   *The Age of Innocence*

F. Scott Fitzgerald   *The Great Gatsby*

Virginia Woolf   *A Room of One's Own*

Robert Cormier   *After the First Death*

Caryl Churchill   *The After-Dinner Joke*
and *Three More Sleepless Nights*

Graham Swift   *Learning to Swim*

Fay Weldon   *Letters to Alice*

Louise Lawrence   *Children of the Dust*

Julian Barnes   *A History of the World in 10½ Chapters*

Amy Tan   *The Joy Luck Club*

Four Women Poets

Moments of Madness – 150 years of short stories

Helen Edmundson   *The Mill on the Floss*